DATE
6

Denial

Denial

DAVID BELBIN

*Hodder
Children's
Books*

A division of Hodder Headline Limited

First published in Great Britain in 2004
by Hodder Children's Books

A Catalogue record for this book is available from
the British Library

ISBN 0 340 87392 2

Typeset in Palatino by Avon DataSet Ltd,
Bidford-on-Avon, Warwickshire

Printed and bound in Great Britain by
Bookmarque Ltd, Croydon, Surrey

The paper and board used in this paperback by
Hodder Children's Books are natural recyclable products
made from wood grown in sustainable forests.
The manufacturing processes conform to the environmental
regulations of the country of origin.

Hodder Children's Books
a division of Hodder Headline Ltd
338 Euston Road
London NW1 3BH

For Michael Eaton

1

The way I see it, most girls my age choose to disconnect sometimes from their mums and/or dads, from their so-called friends, from their screwed-up selves. Dissociation is a skill, or an art. It's what I did during my parents' break-up and it's the way I acted during most of Years Eight and Nine, when all my skanky friends turned on me.

But I'm not like that any more, not since (a) my parents separated for good three years ago and (b) I left behind the losers at my old school and moved in with Dan.

My campaign lasted all last summer. Mum was busy with her new baby and her new husband. Even so, she didn't want to let me go. Then I spent an entire fortnight in the Dordogne being an utter, complete pain. Halfway through, Trevor persuaded Mum to fold. I overheard the two of them talking one night, when I was meant to be asleep but had sneaked out to the patio for a smoke.

'Would it be so bad if she lived with Dan?'

'You don't know what he's like.'

'Caitlin does. And you say he seems to have changed.'

'He doesn't drink when Cate's around,' Mum admitted.

'I looked up the school where he works on the web. It gets great results, much better than where she is now.'

'We don't even know if he could get her in.'

'But if he could . . . ? It'd take a lot of pressure off us.'

'It's not just about us.'

'And it might be the making of Caitlin. We'd still see her weekends, holidays . . .'

'The way she is at the moment, once a month would be quite sufficient.'

Then Trevor laughed and I returned to my room, relieved but not yet relaxed. Before making my escape, I still had to convince Dan, get him to persuade his school to let me go there.

Three weeks later, he did.

'I had to do some serious arm twisting,' he told me

at the end of August, when he came to collect me. 'I've only been there a year, and it's a very popular school.'

'Will the other teachers know I'm your daughter?'

'The head, the head of Year Ten and your form tutor will have to know. Everybody else – I'll leave it up to you when you tell them. Your mother and I thought it best if she did the parents' evenings. You don't want kids teasing you about me.'

'Or vice versa.'

My dad is thirty-six but could pass for twenty-nine. Mum's the same age as him but looks about forty (that's what having a late baby does to you – I'm never having children, never). Dan's most recent girlfriend was a newly qualified teacher at his school, Jo. Age twenty-three. I'll bet he never told her how old he was. Dan's a cool dude, a big head, a top bloke or a trendy tosser – I've heard him called all sorts. He's the sort of person everybody has an opinion about. I'm not sure whether that's a good or a bad thing. At least he's not bland, boring.

'Of course, when you make friends, it's bound to come out.'

'A friend isn't a friend unless she can keep a secret.'

Dan nodded. We were alone in the front room of Mum and Trevor's cottage in Parwich. This was the first time that Dan had been there. Mum was looking around to see if I'd left anything behind. Trevor was in the kitchen, changing baby Daisy. Dan looked at the chintzy decor.

'I didn't know your mum was so into Laura Ashley.'

'The wallpaper's the least of it,' I said. 'I hate—'

Then Mum came in, holding a dust covered Chili Peppers CD she'd found under the bed. Time to go. Time to start being me again: a sharper, cooler, calmer me.

2

My dad had a two-bedroomed, terraced house a couple of miles from Sheffield city centre. It was less than half the size of Mum and Trevor's designer 'cottage', with a tiny yard in place of a garden. But I liked it. There was a lock on my door. I wasn't allowed one in Parwich because, Mum argued, I was a deep sleeper and suppose the wooden beams caught fire? At Dan's I liked the way that the knocked-through living-room walls were lined with shelves full of books and old records (Dan says CDs don't sound real, though he still has hundreds of them, too).

Dan moved to Sheffield last summer. Before that, he taught in London for a year. He had a room in a shared house ('like a student' he used to say, 'at thirty-three and a third!'). I could never stay with him. I'm not sure Mum would have let me go anyhow (they never married, so Dan had no access rights, not unless he went to court, which he couldn't afford to do).

Even after he moved to Sheffield, I didn't visit Dan at home, not at first. The place needed doing up and it was three separate bus journeys away. We met just off the M1, at the Meadowhall shopping centre, or he'd come over to Derby, armpit of the Midlands, which was sort of halfway.

It was March before I visited his home. When Dan brought me back from the bus station, skinny, short-haired Jo was there, planting up pots in the back yard.

'You're the same age as my sister,' she told me. 'We'll get on like a house on fire.'

And we might have done, if it weren't that a few weeks later, Jo got back together with her university boyfriend, who she'd split up with six months before. He'd suddenly realised he couldn't live without her and persuaded Jo to dump Dan, leave her job at Easter, move back south and marry him.

'She told me she was on the big rebound,' Dan told me, on my next monthly visit. 'I didn't want to get too serious. I took her at her word. Always a big mistake with women.'

That afternoon, as we drove from Parwich to Sheffield, I didn't ask about Jo and whether the wedding had gone ahead. Too touchy a subject. Dan only opened up about stuff when he felt like it. And then there were always gaps I was expected to fill in. Or not talk about, anyhow.

'Are you seeing anyone?' I worked up the nerve to ask as we turned onto his road. I needed to know if I'd be sharing him.

'Not any more,' he muttered.

We pulled up outside the house, which is on a kind of cul-de-sac, backing onto a graveyard.

'What about you? Do you have someone back in Derbyshire?'

'Yeah, right. There's this great guy in Year Eleven who's gonna post me poems and take me for long, romantic walks every other weekend.'

'No need to be sarcastic. You're at an age when—'

'Dan, I'd rather kill myself than go out with any of the boys from my old school.'

'Don't say that. We had a boy last year who—'

'Sorry, sorry.'

We went inside. Dan had finally got around to decorating my room for me. He'd not done a bad job. The backing paper was only crooked in one place and there weren't too many bits where the blue paint had run. Posters would hide the flaws, once I knew what kind of posters to put up. I hadn't decided on my new identity yet. It was Friday and school started on Tuesday. Tomorrow Dan was taking me shopping in all the best places. I had three days to make myself up, to become the person I meant to be, the one who would meet the boy, get the grades and leave behind everything that was wrong about me.

3

'Are you letting it grow?'

'Yeah.'

'You've got such a lovely face. Why hide it?'

I hate it when hairdressers act like they know more than you, especially since if they had two GCSEs to rub together, they wouldn't be hairdressers. The whole point of my hair in the last year had been to hide my face. Since the doctor persuaded Mum to put me on the pill though, my skin has cleared up.

I liked having clear skin. I used to have several piercings (two nose, lip, eyebrow, three on each ear). But the school where Dan works is strict – you are only allowed one stud per ear lobe, tops, which isn't worth bothering with. So I've gone for a kind of classic simplicity: clothes plain, but not cheap – dark jeans, soft sweaters and push-up bra to emphasise my 32C boobs. I wasn't going to be a Goth any more. I wasn't sure what to be, except, maybe, mysterious. I let the hairdresser cut my straight, dark-brown hair away from my face – but not too much – keeping it long, only allowing her to tidy up the edges.

'There. What do you think?'

'It's fine,' I grunt. 'Thanks, Tracy.'

And it was fine. For once in my life, I almost liked the way I looked. I even told her to keep the change (Dan's change).

'Cate?' Dan was waiting in the car. 'You look great. I told you Tracy was good, didn't I? Jo used to swear by her.'

It made me uncomfortable to hear him talk about Jo, even though they'd split up. Then I caught my image in the rear-view mirror as I got in the van. I looked two years younger than I did at the end of last term. The marks from my piercings had finished fading. I felt nearly new. Used, maybe, but nearly new.

4

First impressions of my new school. The kids looked a bit older, acted a bit harder. I wouldn't know whether they were more or less well off than at my old school – you couldn't sport many designer labels because there was a strict uniform code. Some of the girls wore a little make-up, very discreet. Nobody seemed interested in me. I got a couple of 'You new?'s. Nobody asked where I came from: asking too many questions wasn't cool.

Some of the boys in the tutor group clowned around, throwing stuff, teasing each other. They stopped as soon as the form tutor came in. Ms Jackson read out the register, including my name. This was when everyone would make their first, instant judgment of me. I played it carefully, managing only a strangulated 'Here'.

'As you'll see, we have a new addition to our form, Caitlin Harris, who recently arrived from

Derbyshire. What do you like to be called, Caitlin?'

'Don't mind,' I said. 'Caitlin or Cate, whatever.'

'Then I shall use your full name.'

I preferred Cate, pronounced 'Kate', though it led to confusion over how my name was spelt, followed by questions about whether I'd changed the spelling to copy some Australian actress. As for Caitlin, I liked the suggestion of Irishness, even though nobody in any part of my family was Irish. Harris is my mother's maiden name and is kind of safe. My dad's surname is Fordham, which is OK, but doesn't go with Caitlin.

'Holly, will you show Caitlin where everything is?'

'Sure, Miss.'

I was handed to the care of a short, bespectacled girl who wore a school sweater. She moved her chair next to mine then talked me through my timetable printout at great speed. Unlike some in the class, she had a thick Yorkshire accent, and it took me a while to tune in to what she was saying.

'Mr Green for English, that's not so good. I've got Mr Fordham. He's lush. Taylor for Art, you could do worse . . .'

I hoped I hadn't flushed when she mentioned Dan. Holly didn't seem to spot any weirdness on my part, just kept on going on about other teachers. She was a little long-sighted so got close to the paper, which meant I could look over her head and check out the rest of the form. This lot had been together for three years, so I'd already missed six hundred episodes of a weekday soap concerning their alliances and fallings-out, the bullying, bribery, thwarted ambitions and endless humiliations.

'Whydyumovere?'

Hardly anybody had an accent at my old school. I began to worry that I might have to develop one if I wanted to fit in.

'Sorry?' As soon as I'd said this, I worked out what she said: *Why did you move here?*

'Divorce job?'

I nodded, but I didn't rush to add details, the way girls-who-are-going-to-be-best-mates would. So Holly didn't confide whatever she was on the edge of confiding.

'Thought so,' was all she said. 'It's in your eyes.'

5

I first saw him on my second day. He was lanky, with curly, longish fair hair and an appealingly relaxed face. The girl he was walking alongside was about my height, five four, with a skirt two inches shorter than regulation, showing off fantastic legs. She wore a little eye shadow and had slightly chubby cheeks. Yet I could see she was glamorous. If this boy, who had warm, brown eyes, fancied her, he wasn't going to fancy me.

They had to be in Year Eleven. I could have told him that great looking girls in Year Eleven don't go out with guys from the same year. They want blokes with cars and money – or at least somebody from the Sixth Form College where you don't have to wear uniform. I turned on my invisibility shield and tagged along behind them.

'I'll help you with it if you want,' he was saying.

'OK.'

'Shall I come round to yours?'

'No. Library after school.'

The boy looked sullen – helping someone in the school library was hardly a date. But it was a result for me. The library stayed open until four thirty. Dan couldn't be sure when he would get away in the evening so he'd said that he'd always look for me there before going.

Getting home on my own was a pain. Dan lived outside the school catchment area and there was no school bus. I had to get a bus into town then another one out again, which involved a massive detour. But I didn't want to be seen with Dan, not at first, anyhow. That morning, he'd dropped me half a mile from school and I'd walked the rest, careful not to arrive too early.

The tall boy was in the library when I got there. Alone. He was trying to look cool, reading the *Daily Mirror* but glancing over the top of the paper every time anybody walked by. So when he glanced at me, the expression I caught was disappointment. I walked over to the newspaper stand and picked up a copy of *The Independent*. It was probably only there for the teachers. We got *The Guardian* delivered at home, along with *Heat* and *J17* for me and *Q* for Dan. Neither of my parents read tabloids, so I'd decided that they were beneath me, too. But there was nothing in the broadsheet that interested me. Five minutes later, when the lanky lad put down the *Mirror*, I spoke to him.

'Have you finished with that?'

'Sure. I'll swap you.'

We exchanged newspapers and he gave me a friendly smile.

'I'm Aaron,' he said.

'Caitlin.'

'Waiting for someone?'

I had to come up with a quick explanation, but didn't want to fib, not in our first conversation. 'My dad picks me up when he finishes work, so I thought I'd kill time here.'

Aaron nodded. 'Where'd you live?'

'Out of catchment. By Abbeyfield Park. You?'

'Pitsmoor. We're practically neighbours.'

'Why do you come here?' I asked him.

'We lived up the road until my parents split up. Then they both had to move somewhere cheaper.'

We exchanged the basic details. Aaron lived with his mum, who was single, while his dad had a new partner and baby. We were like opposite sides of the

16

same coin. And he lived near me. I was on such a buzz. Then Aaron looked over my shoulder and I remembered why he was there in the first place.

'Natasha? Is something wrong?'

'I need to get out of here. Will you walk me?'

'Sure.'

And Aaron walked out, a protective arm around the short-skirted girl, without even saying goodbye to me.

6

Dan turned up five minutes later and had a quick word with the librarian. I waited until two minutes after he'd gone, then followed him out to the camper van. Aaron and Natasha were long gone. Most of the staff had left too, so we weren't likely to be seen. But the VW van was really distinctive. I didn't want to be noticed, so sat in the back, with its smoked windows and fold-down beds. I perched myself against the doors, trying to dredge up happy memories of the pop festivals Mum and Dan took me to when I was a kid.

Dan didn't speak at all during the long, stop-start drive. He looked preoccupied. I figured this was Dan in work mode, tired by a long day. When we got home, I watched TV. Dan dozed, then did some lesson preparation. I would have forgotten the entire evening were it not for what happened the next day.

Before dinner, I took twenty minutes to do my Maths

homework, my first homework at my new school. We ate while watching the *Channel Four News*. At seven thirty, I turned over to watch *Coronation Street*. After that, I spent half an hour on the internet, reading blogs. Most of the diaries I read were by girls with lives as messed-up as mine. You could post a comment, but I never did. Who was I to offer advice to a seventeen-year-old with no boyfriend? I tried to imagine what it would be like to go out with tall, skinny Aaron. Then Dan called me. I disconnected and we watched a movie he was thinking of using in his teaching.

Dan was keen. He kept stopping the tape and making notes, asking me questions, mentioning things he was going to look up on the internet. I was beginning to see: kids didn't only like Dan because they fancied him, like Holly. He was good at his job, too. I felt mixed up about this: glad but kind of annoyed. They'd been getting more out of him than I had.

Just after I went to bed, around half ten, the phone rang. Dan picked up and I fell asleep.

Next day it was raining so I went all the way into school with Dan, pulling my old hooded jacket up over my head as I ran from the back of the VW van to registration. Why was my paranoia-count so low? Because I was picking-up how popular a teacher Dan was. People knowing I was his daughter might not be such a bad thing.

I sensed something as soon as school started but didn't interpret the atmosphere until later: gossip, spreading like a super-virus. Holly picked up a version of events at morning break and relayed it to me in Maths.

'They're saying a girl in Year Nine got raped by a boy in Year Eleven after school last night. He's been arrested.'

'Who?' Not that either name would have meant anything to me.

'Dunno.'

By lunchtime, the story went that a Year Eleven girl had been raped in one of the Year Nine common rooms.

'By a Year Eleven boy?' I asked in afternoon registration.

Holly lowered her voice. 'A teacher.'

I flinched. 'Which one?'

'Dunno. What's the betting it all gets hushed up, anyhow?'

* * *

That afternoon, it was still raining so everybody stayed inside. The crowded corridors were full of whispered conversations and speculation. Names were bandied about: any girl who was absent might have been the victim. There were no male teachers missing, so the whole male staff was under suspicion.

I had an advantage over everybody else. My dad was a teacher at the school. Come home-time, I would find out the full story, or as much of it as Dan knew and felt able to tell.

I waited for him in the library after school. When he hadn't shown by four thirty, I checked that the camper van was still in the car park. It was. Then I went to the Year Nine common room which doubled as his form room. Locked.

The library was closing. I couldn't ask the librarian for help – I didn't want her knowing my business. I ran Dan's mobile. Switched off. I thought about getting the bus into town and out again but that seemed stupid – it was nearly rush hour and the journey would take forever.

Walking down the corridor that led to the admin block I turned a corner and almost collided with the younger of the school's two caretakers. He wore a badge telling me his name was Michael.

21

'You haven't seen Mr Fordham, have you?' I asked.

He gave me a funny look, or maybe it was a normal expression for him. Holly said he was a little 'touched'.

'Got you in detention, has he?'

'Not exactly. I have to see him is all.'

'Take my advice,' the caretaker said. 'It's late. Go home.'

So that was what I did, going home the long, two-bus way because I didn't have the five quid a cab would have cost.

It was nearly six when I got in. Dan wasn't there. I ran myself a bath. I wasn't worried, not really. Dan could be flakey sometimes. The bath was hot and deep. I fell asleep in it, not waking until I heard the door slam downstairs. I got out of the bath and called downstairs.

'Dan? Is everything all right?'

No reply. By the time I'd put on my dressing gown and made it downstairs, he had opened a bottle of Russian vodka and was putting ice in a glass. It was three years since I'd seen him drink.

'Sorry, love,' he said to me. 'It's been a bitch of a day.'

The phone rang before I could ask him anything else.

'Thanks for getting back to me so quickly . . . no,

they haven't, not formally . . . The head said he had to get hold of the Chair of Governors . . . No reason I'm aware of but you know what girls that age . . . if you think I should, I will . . . thanks, that's a comfort, Barry . . . I'll see you tomorrow.'

The conversation lasted about ten minutes. I could hear it from my bedroom as I dried off and dressed. When I got back downstairs, Dan was pouring himself another vodka.

'What's wrong?' I asked.

Dan sighed. 'Barry Grogan from the union says this happens all the time. Or, at least, a lot more often than you think.'

'What?'

'A girl in Year Eleven's made an allegation about me. It's not clear exactly what she said, the head won't tell me.'

'She's saying you raped her?'

'Where did you get that idea?' Dan said sharply. Then he sighed. 'The head said there'd be all kinds of rumours. I take it they've started already. But all I know is that I'm meant to have committed some kind of an assault.'

'She says you hit her?' I couldn't imagine Dan hitting anybody.

'Sexual assault.'

What was the difference between rape and sexual assault? I didn't know.

'Why would anyone do something like that?'

'I have no idea. She always seemed pretty normal to me.'

'What's her name?'

'I don't think I ought to tell you.'

For a moment, I thought this answer was suspicious. He hadn't denied it yet.

'Did you do anything to her?' I asked. 'Anything at all?'

'Nothing. Cate, I swear. You have to believe me on this. Whatever she's saying, she's made the whole thing up.'

I chose to believe him, totally. He was too upset to be lying. If we did hugs, this is where I should have given him one. But I was getting concerned about the gossip.

'It'll be all over school tomorrow,' I said.

'Hopefully the girl will think better of it overnight.'

'If she doesn't,' I said, hot-headed, 'I'll beat the—'

'NO! That behaviour is why you moved schools. This will all blow over by the weekend. Don't try to find out who the girl is.'

I already knew who she was. Or thought I knew. I had her name, her first name at least: Natasha.

7

'This seat free?' a mild voice asked. I nodded without really looking, preoccupied by Dan's situation. That morning, he'd woken me early, told me I had to get the bus to school. He was going in later. I suspected he hadn't slept.

'I thought you got a lift?' It was Aaron. My head clicked into gear.

'Dad doesn't have time to take me every morning.'

'Sorry I hurried off the other day.'

''S'OK. Your girlfriend showed up.'

'Natasha's not my girlfriend. She's . . . a friend who's having problems.'

Bet you wish she was your girlfriend. For a moment, I thought I'd said this aloud, but I hadn't. I began to calculate.

'What kind of problems?' I asked.

Aaron looked away. 'How do you like the school?'

'Too early to say.'

'Found much to do in Burngreave?'

'Not yet. I've only lived there a couple of weeks.'

'Want to go out one night, get a burger or something?'

'Sure.'

He smiled and only then did he look at me again. *So I guess Natasha really isn't your girlfriend I thought. Otherwise you wouldn't have asked me out. Did you really do that?* No boy ever asked me out at my old school, except as a joke. This wasn't a joke, was it? Aaron seemed to be waiting for me to say something else.

'Do you want my mobile number?' I gave it to him. Then we arrived at school and went our separate ways. If it weren't for what was happening to Dan, I'd have been on top of the world.

Things move on quickly in schools. Since there were no more details of the 'rape' the day before, nobody in Year Ten was talking about it, though I heard three Year Eights gossiping outside the Year Nine common room.

'Was it someone in our year?'

'I heard Year Nine.'

'My sister said it was a girl in Year Eleven and Michael the moron.'

At least nobody was mentioning my dad. Maybe he was right and it would all be over by the weekend.

Everything looks different depending whose point of view you see it from. According to Dan, that's one of the main things you learn in English. It's almost the whole point of English Literature: there's no such thing as objectivity, everything's subjective. You never find out what really happened to anyone else, ever. Which makes you want to know all the more.

I didn't want to desert Dan at the end of Friday, so waited in the library after school. That was where Aaron found me.

'Thought you'd be here again,' he said. 'Your dad collecting you?'

'Yeah.' What would I do if Aaron wanted a lift?

'Doing anything this weekend?'

'Not a lot.' This was my weekend to stay in Burngreave. 'Maybe you could show me the local sights.'

'Only if you've got a whole five minutes to spare.'

As he said this, Dan walked in. Aaron saw him first and his face, normally slack, seemed to tighten. 'I'll call you tonight,' he said, and left.

I looked round. Dan was checking that the coast was clear. I was the only person in the library except for the librarian, who was at a computer screen with her back to us, as usual. Dan whispered.

'Sorry, love. I've got to see the head. My union rep's coming along. We're going to try and fix this nonsense from yesterday. Here, get a taxi home.'

I took the fiver, then got out my mobile as if calling a taxi. When Dan left, I put it away again. I hurried out to join Aaron at the bus stop, getting there just as the bus was pulling out. It waited for me and I joined Aaron at the back.

'Sorry I rushed off like that,' he said.

''S'all right. You had a bus to catch.'

'Why're you here?'

'My dad just rang to say he was running late.'

There were only a handful of other school kids on the bus. I could talk to Aaron without feeling ridiculously self-conscious. For the next few minutes, I got him to talk about himself. All the magazines say that's the best way to get into a boy's good books, not to go all girly or giggly or gossipy on them. I found out what bands he liked, how much he hated sport (all sport! Just like me!) and that he had a sister called Melanie.

When we got to town, there was a bus in but we didn't hurry to take it.

'The bus up the Wicker's really slow this time of day,' Aaron said. 'Want to walk it?'

'Why not?' It was sunny and only a little cool. But the walk was all uphill. I had trouble keeping up with Aaron, whose legs were so much longer than mine. At first the walk took us by run-down shops and flats. As the road got steeper, the buildings grew smarter. I ran out of questions, so had to tell Aaron some of the things he wanted to know, like what my old school was like.

'A cess pit. That's the main reason I moved here. I mean, my dad's all right, but it was more that I just had to get away . . .'

I felt like I'd betrayed Dan when I said that, but I hadn't moved here for him. I'd only been in Sheffield five days and already missed Mum, and Daisy. Dan's school seemed better than my old one, but my main reason for moving was to escape my so-called 'friends' at Ashbourne Comp. I started explaining this to Aaron, trying not to make myself sound too screwed-up or needy.

'Don't you turn off somewhere round here?' I asked, after getting carried away with a description of the bitchiness of the Year Nine cliques at my old school.

'Two streets back,' Aaron said with a grin. 'I'll walk you to the door.'

I let him. These streets weren't exactly the safest in Sheffield and Dan wouldn't be home yet. As we turned off the main road, Aaron looked at the park.

'Wish I lived round here.'

'I'm sure your house is nice.'

'No. It's not.'

'I'd invite you in, only I haven't mentioned you to my dad and . . .'

'Don't worry. I'd better get going. I'll call you in the morning, OK?'

'OK. I'd like that.'

We paused a few houses from my front door. For at least a second, neither of us moved. I was turning to go when Aaron leant forward and, barely touching me, planted a kiss on my cheek. I didn't know what to do or say.

'Bye.' I watched him walk down the street for at least five seconds before realising that he might turn round. I'd better go inside if I didn't want to look like a love-struck fool.

Dan didn't get home for another two hours. He'd been suspended.

8

On Saturday, when Dan finally got up, he was in good shape. You wouldn't think that he'd been playing music so loudly it woke me: the Clash, Big Black and finally, on repeat: *Smells Like Teen Spirit*, until two when the neighbours came and complained.

I could hear him from my room at the front of the house, apologising profusely. Dan was always popular when drunk. He didn't get violent or angry or fall over. All he did was play music too loudly and bring home unsuitable friends. None of that bothered me when he lived with Mum. Even if it had, he did most of his drinking after I'd gone to bed.

At Primary School, my friends were envious: I had a fun dad. He worked as an actor before training to be a teacher. Not very successfully. His longest stint was an eighteen-month Theatre in Education touring production about drugs. But he was in a couple of TV ads, which meant big kudos with my friends.

His drinking got worse on that long tour, away from home during the week, every week. He'd turned thirty and wasn't going to make it, not big-time. He was too handsome for Mr Ordinary parts on soaps, not handsome enough to be a leading man. He didn't look like a villain either. He looked like a teacher.

While Dan was away on tour, Mum started seeing Trevor. His wife had left him and he needed a bit of looking after, she said (not that she told me a lot, I was only eleven and not supposed to wonder why Trevor kept coming round. But I heard what Mum told Dan. He seemed to believe her. Maybe it was true at first).

Trevor was Mum's boss. When they started seeing each other openly, Mum had to move departments (the council had strict rules about stuff like that). There was a really messy period where Mum tried to throw Dan out of the house, but Dan wouldn't go. Then Dan did throw Mum out and Mum moved in with Trevor.

I stayed with Dan, who wouldn't accept that his relationship with Mum was over. He got through two bottles of vodka a day during that time. I used to see the empties in the morning. Sometimes he'd still be slumped in an armchair when I got up to go to school.

One of his Pink Floyd or Joy Division records would still be spinning round on the turntable. The record was old, so the needle just got stuck at the end, wearing out the final groove. That was when the acting work dried up altogether. Then Mum stopped paying the rent on the house. Dan got into arrears and moved out just before we were evicted.

Since Mum and Dan never married, there was no need for a divorce. Mum married Trevor as soon as his came through. Why she married him when she'd refused to get hitched to Dan I don't know. The only time I asked, she said:

'Dan was never husband material, Cate. I loved him. I still love him. But it always felt like I had two children.'

Mum and Trevor moved to Parwich, a boring Peak District village in between Ashbourne and Bakewell. Driving into the village, you pass this sign: *Changed Priorities Ahead*. When we first moved there, Trevor used to joke about it. Three years on, the sign's still there. And I want to know: when does changed become normal?

Dan knew he wouldn't get custody of me, not officially. He agreed to every other weekend and one two-week holiday a year. Then he started his teacher training course. Mum had persuaded him to apply back when they were together. He didn't really want to do it but the bursary was better than the dole. The only way for him to get through the course was to stop drinking. Having done that, he discovered, to his surprise, that he was very good at teaching.

'It's acting all day,' he told me. 'But the part's for real and the pay's much better. I think I was made to do this.'

That was two years ago, when he was working in London. According to him, the school in Sheffield was even better.

'I can do this for the rest of my life,' he'd told me, and I was happy for him.

That Saturday morning, Dan acted cheerful, but it wasn't like our shopping expedition of the week before. It was as though we were only doing stuff so I'd be able to tell Mum about it when she rang. Dan took me to the Yorkshire Sculpture Park, where we walked among Henry Moore sculptures, avoiding sheep shit, trying to make small talk.

I thought being suspended was something that only happened to kids. But, according to Dan, the head and governors had no choice but to suspend him on full pay until the situation was sorted out – it didn't mean they believed the allegation. Dan was seeing Barry Grogan, a teachers' union official, the next day and there was no more to say about it. But we had nothing else to talk about, so we barely talked at all. The weather turned. We drove to Crystal Peaks, a multiplex just outside the city centre. Dan let me choose the film.

Aaron hadn't phoned before I went out. I'd given him my mobile number, but I didn't have his, so couldn't let him know I'd be out with Dad all day. As soon as we left Crystal Peaks, I checked to see who'd called. Only Mum.

When we got home, Dan cooked pasta, but he didn't drink, not a drop. As far as I could tell, there was no booze in the house. The last two nights had been a freak event, an aberration, in response to stress.

Aaron rang at nine the next morning.

'Sorry I didn't call yesterday. Something came up. Can I see you today?'

'I guess. Where do you want to meet?'

'I could come round to yours.'

'Not a good idea. How about the cemetery, just inside the gates, in an hour?'

He was already there when I arrived. *What kind of girl arranges a first date in the local cemetery?* he must have been thinking. I hoped he'd kiss me, but he didn't. Nor did he explain what had happened the day before. He was wearing jeans and a fleece that was practically pink. Either he had weird taste or his mum still bought most of his clothes for him.

'Want to walk around?'

'Sure.'

He didn't try to hold my hand. Maybe I'd misinterpreted Friday's kiss on the cheek. He wanted to be my friend, not my boyfriend. We walked around the gravestones, occasionally making strained, silly jokes. It started to rain.

'Where's your house?' Aaron asked. 'Over there?'

'Yeah. But my dad might be . . . funny about you coming in.'

'Have you had a boyfriend before?'

'Not really. Have you had a girlfriend?'

'Not a serious one.'

I tried not to blush. From friend to girlfriend to potential serious girlfriend in the space of a minute. I guess I must have gazed at him doe-eyed or given him some kind of mushy come-on because the next thing I knew he was kissing me. The kiss lasted for ages and, by the time it was over, the rain had stopped.

9

Dan gave me a lift into school on Monday, dropping me on a quiet corner.

'I don't want what's happening to spoil things for you. It's going to blow over by the end of the week. The girl will think better of it, I'm sure.'

'But why is she doing it? What's she got against you?'

Dan hesitated. 'It's best not to speculate. Don't shoot your mouth off, Cate. I don't want you getting involved.'

'I'm not going to tell anyone anything about you. I just want to know why this mad cow is making—'

Dan put a finger to my lips. 'We're talking about a troubled young woman. Maybe she's taking revenge for some imagined crime. Maybe she's somehow convinced herself that something happened. You can't get inside other people's heads, Cate. Sometimes it's stupid even to try. Now, go and do your best at school.'

He was right. This was to be my first full week and I ought to make the best of it.

Despite what was going on, I was kind of looking forward to school, in a way I hadn't since Infants.

Holly found me at morning break, after we'd both had English (in different groups).

'We had a supply teacher for English.'

'So?'

'Mr Fordham didn't teach our lesson on Friday, either. But he was in school.'

'Maybe he's on a course,' I said. 'Or doing interviews.'

Holly gave me an odd look, like she'd sussed that I was a teacher's daughter.

'Or maybe he's in trouble,' she suggested. 'Sam Goody says she saw him going into the head's office on Friday.'

By morning break, everybody in Year Ten somehow knew exactly who and what was involved:

'He tried to rape Natasha Clark in the Year Nine common room after school last Wednesday, that's what they're saying.'

'He didn't rape her. My sister knows Nat. She says he

felt her up and asked her for a blow job, but Nat blew the whistle on him.'

'She's a right slag, Natasha Clark. Everyone knows she had an abortion in Year Ten. He probably thought she was asking for it.'

Nobody even considered that the teacher's accuser might have made the whole thing up.

'Do you know this Natasha?' I asked Holly at lunch.

'Only by reputation.'

'What's her reputation, then?'

'In Year Nine, she'd shag anything that moved, mostly boys in Year Eleven. By Year Ten, she calmed down. Some people reckoned it was because she'd had an abortion. Or maybe it was because she could pass for twenty and started seeing older blokes who treated her properly.'

'Do you think Mr Fordham . . . ?'

'You must be kidding,' Holly said. 'Mr Fordham wouldn't go for a slapper like Natasha. He used to go out with Miss Grant, who was this young, great-looking teacher. Then she got another job. Nah, I reckon Natasha's got it in for him for some reason.'

I tried to look like I was enjoying the gossip but, inside, I was nervy. I stopped asking questions before

Holly sensed anything strange. I knew better than to take everything she said at face value. The stuff about Jo Grant was true enough, but the dirt on Natasha might not be. I'd had enough lies told about me to know that.

During afternoon registration, Sam Goody asked our form teacher straight out: 'Is it true Mr Fordham's been sacked for feeling up Natasha Clark, Ms Jackson?'

The teacher looked flustered. 'I don't want to hear people spreading stories like that.'

'Even if they're true?' a loud lad called out.

'Quiet!' Ms Jackson restored order than spoke calmly. 'There is a ... a situation involving Mr Fordham and neither I, nor any of your other teachers are allowed to discuss it with you. So, please, get to your classes.'

As we were leaving, Ms Jackson tapped me on the shoulder.

'Caitlin, hang on. There's a form I need you to fill in.' When we were alone, she continued, 'How are you coping, Caitlin?'

I stared at the floor. I hardly knew Ms J and I hated that she knew who my dad was.

'If you need to talk about this to anyone ...'

I shook my head slowly. 'He didn't do what this girl's accusing him of. There isn't anything else to say.'

Ms Jackson's voice became warmer, softer. 'I'm sure you're right, Caitlin. The staff all feel the same way, but, of course, no-one's allowed to say anything. It seems terribly unfair.'

She was trying to appear kind but her smile was awkward.

'Can I go now?' I asked, politely.

'Yes.' She seemed at once disappointed and relieved.

10

I got the bus home with Aaron. I wanted to tell him that it was my dad who'd been suspended, but thought it might put him off. Also, despite the previous afternoon, I didn't yet know if I could trust him. He might tell his mates (or, worse, Natasha) that I was Mr Fordham's daughter.

On the second bus, he held my hand.

'Do you want to go home?' Aaron asked, when we were near his stop.

'Not really.'

'Come to mine, then.'

'OK.' I'd never been to a boy's house and would rather I wasn't in my school uniform: the green blazer and boring grey skirt were hardly attractive. But Aaron was in uniform too.

'Will your mum be there?'

'Just my sister. Mum doesn't get back from work until six.'

That meant we had over ninety minutes to ourselves, ninety minutes when I could try to forget what was happening to Dan.

His house was up the hill on the left, just beyond the flats, on Rising Street. It was smaller than Dan's, but better decorated. Aaron's room was a tiny attic conversion and very hot, even when we opened the dormer window. I'd bet it got cold in winter. He put a Belle and Sebastian CD on. Then we kissed.

At first, Aaron kissed me too hard, as though he was attacking me with his tongue. And he couldn't decide what to do with his hands. The whole thing felt awkward, more like I was being attacked than embraced. Then, just as I was getting uncomfortable, he began to calm down. Our tongues sloshed around each other. His right hand settled under my sweater, gently squeezing my left breast through my thin cotton bra.

The boys at my old school looked at me like I was dirt or worse. That afternoon, I was so grateful for Aaron's attention, I would have let him go further than I really wanted. But he backed off without even undoing my bra.

'Show me something.' I said.

'Like what?'

'I dunno.' Not used to being treated with respect, I felt relaxed, flippant. 'Your books, CDs . . . no, tell you what – show me your clothes. I'll tell you which ones I like and which ones I don't. Then you'll know what to wear when I go out with you.'

'OK,' Aaron said. Getting into the idea, he began pulling our drawers. 'Fine. I'll start with this.'

He found a purple, grandad-vest type top that was so small he could barely get it on. We both giggled. He had a nice chest, a few hairs emerging between his prominent ribs.

'Never let me see you in that again! Now, something else.'

He produced an enormous Shetland wool sweater which made him look pregnant, then a Spice Girls T-shirt that his sister had bought him as a joke. Aaron must have run through at least a dozen shirts and trousers, the two of us laughing harder and harder as the choices and combinations became more bizarre.

The worst thing he owned (he made me look away before putting them on) was a pair of acrylic Y-fronts in navy blue with a light blue trim. I made him keep them on and perform for me. The Chemical Brothers were turned up loud and Aaron was dancing around the room in these underpants when the door shot open and his mother walked in, still in her supermarket uniform. The Y-fronts didn't seem to faze her.

'Aaron, why the hell are you making so much . . . ?'

Then she saw me and her face changed from confusion to thunder. 'Put some clothes on and bring your guest downstairs NOW!'

11

'Maybe you ought to move back in with your mum.'

'No! Why on earth should I do that?'

'Because things are going to be ugly here for a while. People are bound to find out that you're my daughter. That'll make things hard for you at school.'

'Why should they find out? Ms Jackson's not letting on. I haven't told anybody.'

'Nobody at all?'

'I wasn't going to tell anybody until I was comfortable.'

'What about this boy you've been seeing?'

'I haven't told him, either.'

'But he's the main reason you want to stay.'

'No!' I lied. 'I want to stay because you need my support.'

Dan smiled, pretending to believe this. 'But listen, once your mum finds out, she won't want you living with me.'

'Mum's not going to believe you did it.'

'Are you sure?'

'Yes. She believes in you.' Mum never said bad stuff about Dan, though he often deserved it. If I tried to criticise him, she'd always take his side, even after she married Trevor.

'If I were her, I wouldn't let you stay with me.'

'OK, then,' I thought fast and aloud. 'I won't tell them. It won't be a lie, just an omission.'

Dan put his head in his hands while he considered this.

'The police want to interview me tomorrow,' he told me.

Before I could say anything, the doorbell rang. Still wearing my school uniform, I answered it. The man at the door was fortyish with a receding hairline. He seemed taken aback to see me.

'I believe Daniel Fordham lives here.' He spoke slightly too quickly.

'Who wants to know?'

'Are you a friend of his?' he asked, cautiously, as Dan came up behind me.

'Who are you?'

'Mr Fordham? I'm Russ Michaels from *The Sheffield Star*. The school has put out a statement about your suspension and I thought you might like to comment on it.'

Dan walked straight into it. 'A statement? I was told that I wasn't going to be named.'

'The statement confirms that a member of staff has been suspended pending an investigation into the incident, but we have our sources too and I wanted to give you the chance to—'

That's when Dan shut the door in his face. But the reporter kept talking.

'You might find it a relief to get your side of the story into print as quickly as possible.'

'No comment,' Dan shouted.

'Who's the girl that answered the door, Mr Fordham? I'm sure there's an innocent explanation but you have to admit it doesn't look good . . .'

'Fuck off!' Dan yelled. My heart sank. Why hadn't he denied it, at least? Dan was straight on the phone to Barry, the union official. He spent the next five minutes blowing off steam. I made a pot of tea, hoping it would calm him down.

'How did they find me?' he ranted. 'The head assured me that this would be anonymous!'

'What did Barry say?' I asked, when Dan got off the phone.

'Reporter probably got my address from the phone book. Evidently, nine times out of ten, in cases like this, somebody tips off the papers.'

'But didn't the head say he wouldn't name you?'

'The school's statement didn't name me. It said the suspension was without prejudice to my future in the school. But the reporter already knew who I was. Everybody in the city's going to know I've been suspended.'

'But will they know what for? Has he talked to Natasha?'

Dan sighed. 'If you've already found out her name, he's bound to. So your mum and Trevor will soon know.'

'It's not national news,' I pointed out.

'Derbyshire's only the next county.'

'But it's not that big a story. Please don't make me go back,' I pleaded. 'Why should I be punished for something you didn't do? It's so unfair!'

'Life isn't fair,' Dan said. But he stopped going on about my moving out.

12

'Where does your dad think you are?' my boyfriend asked.

'With a friend.' Aaron's mum was out and I'd needed to escape from home, where every minute felt like an hour. It was doing my head in.

'A boyfriend?'

'I didn't say. He's OK about me going out as long as I have my mobile on.' I couldn't tell him Dan was happy for me to be seeing Aaron. Aaron couldn't come to the house in case he met Dan, so it was simpler to make my father sound forbidding.

'What shall we do at the weekend?'

'Got to stay at my mum's.'

'I forgot. Think she'd let me come with you one day?'

'Maybe, in time, but I wouldn't hold your breath.'

Mum would probably like Aaron, too, but I couldn't

risk him blabbing about what was happening to a teacher at our school.

'How about Sunday night? What time do you get back?'

'Dunno. I'll call. What are you going to do this weekend?'

'I'll probably see Nat. She's having a rough time.'

'Don't you see enough of her at school?' I said, cautious, not wanting to sound jealous or over-interested. 'I thought she was in your form.'

'She is, but she took all of last week off, waiting for things to calm down.'

'I see.' I hadn't seen Natasha around but thought that was because she'd been doing police and social services interviews.

'Has she told you what happened?' I asked, casually.

'I was the first person she told, right after it happened. I was talking to you in the library when she came in. Remember?'

I chose my next words carefully. 'I don't want to sound nosy but . . . what did she tell you?'

Aaron gave one of his sad, edge-of-lips-curled-down smiles. 'She didn't want to go into any details at first. But as soon as I realised how bad it was, I told her, she had to report him.'

'How bad?'

'Thing is, I may have to talk to the police.'

'Why? You weren't a witness.'

'No, but I can say what state she was in after it happened. Then there's the diary of course.'

'Diary?'

'Yeah. I keep a diary. I've been doing it since I started secondary school. It's pretty detailed.'

I went all girly on him. 'That's brilliant! Can I see?'

'They're just computer files.'

'And you wrote down everything that Natasha said?'

'As soon as I got home.'

'So what does she say that . . . Mr Fordham did, exactly?'

Aaron took his hand off my shoulder. 'She didn't say exactly but I got a pretty strong impression of what he wanted to do, if she'd let him.'

'And you believe her?'

Aaron looked offended. 'Of course. I've been Nat's friend for ten years, and I've never known her tell lies.'

Some guys are incapable of believing that a girl can tell barefaced lies. Especially a pretty one.

13

The story in the newspaper could have been worse. It named Dan, but there was no photograph, no mention of me. The reporter referred to 'unspecified allegations of a sexual nature'. There was no interview with Natasha (according to Dan, they weren't allowed to interview her, because she was under sixteen). The reporter mentioned that Dan's suspension was 'a neutral act' and said the police had yet to bring any charges.

The police didn't seem to be in a hurry. They questioned Dan, with a solicitor present, for half an hour. Afterwards, the officer in charge said they might need to speak to him again.

Dan spent the next few days being upbeat, trying to treat the situation as an unexpected holiday. Every day, when I got back from school, he would tell me what he'd done: dusted and reorganised the books, burned all his computer MP3s onto CD so he could play them on the hi-fi, sorted out some old clothes and taken a load to Oxfam. It was kind of pathetic. By Friday, his cheeriness was wearing me down. I was glad to get away to Mum and Trevor's.

Collecting me, Trevor didn't come in, didn't even speak to Dan. On the way back to Parwich, he asked about the new school, but not once about my father. Either he hadn't heard about the allegation, or he was good at covering up.

'Your mum misses you,' he said, as we drove through Ashbourne. 'You're welcome to come back any time. That comes from me too. I know we've had our problems, but I mean it.'

I didn't reply. When we got in, Daisy was asleep. I had to wait until morning to see her properly. Then I spent most of Saturday playing with her.

'Aren't you going to see Helen?' Mum asked a couple of times. I half-explained that I'd fallen out with my only friend in the village, though I didn't go into why.

On Sunday, while the Indian summer continued, we went on one of Mum's favourite walks, round Lathkill Dale, then had a pub lunch. Dan came to collect me at seven, bang on time. He and Mum had a brief chat. On the way back, Dan told me what it was about.

'Your mother and I agreed that it makes more sense to meet at the services in the middle than it does for each of us to drive the whole way every Friday or Saturday. OK with you?'

'I guess.' If it meant I'd never have to have more than forty minutes of talking to Trevor in the car, it was an improvement. We were out of the village before Dan asked: 'They hadn't heard, then?'

'No. They hadn't heard. Or if they had, they didn't mention it to me. Did anything else happen?'

'No. A couple of teachers rang up to see how I was doing. Evidently the girl's back in school tomorrow.'

'Everybody knows who she is. There's no need to keep pretending she's anonymous.'

'I want you to stay away from her. Sheila told me what you did to those girls at your old school.'

'I've got a temper, but they deserved it.' We were only talking about a few bruises, some torn clothes and a black eye. I can control my temper, but nobody calls me a slag.

'Let's not go into that. But if you threaten or even just try to persuade . . . Natasha . . . to withdraw her story, it could backfire very badly on me. Understood?'

'Understood.'

14

Natasha was in school on Monday. Her hair was cut shorter and her skirt was regulation length. She'd had a makeover from school slut into innocent victim. I tried not to stare but it was hard. She was constantly surrounded by her cronies, keeping the gossips and gigglers at bay. Of course, that only made people talk about her more. The tide was turning in her favour. I've never hated someone so much.

'I think she's so brave, coming back.'

'I hadn't noticed how good looking she was before. Now I can see why Mr Fordham couldn't keep his hands off her.'

'I never believed all those stories about her.'

'Lads exaggerate, that's the trouble. And Mr Fordham probably fell for it, thought she was easy. Then he wouldn't take "no" for an answer. That's what I reckon.'

I bit my lip. At least Aaron wasn't part of Natasha's

entourage. Had he seen her at the weekend? I kept my cool and didn't ask about it until we were on the second bus home.

'Yeah. I went round. She's coping. What's happened to your dad, by the way? It's over a week since he gave you a lift.' This threw me. But before I could answer, Aaron went on, 'Or did you tell him that you preferred getting the bus?'

'If you had a choice between hanging round the library after school every day or riding home with me, what would you choose?'

Aaron grinned, then kissed me. 'Come back to mine?'

'Better not. Dad was really mad I was so late last Monday.'

'My mum's out tomorrow night.'

'I'll see what I can do.'

When I got home, Dan wanted to know what had been said, and by whom.

'They're mostly on your side. But you know what people are like. Some are always ready to believe the worst of anybody.'

'Even plain-speaking Yorkshire folk?' Dan sneered. He had this cynical, sarcastic side that he used to use with Mum, but not with me. Maybe his using it now meant he was treating me as a grown-up, but I didn't like it in him.

'They aren't as bad as the kids at my old school.'

I wanted to talk about Helen – about how, last Easter, when she was on holiday, her sort-of-boyfriend Jason tried to get me drunk and stick his hand down my knickers because he'd heard I was easy. I told him to get lost and when Helen got back Jason told her I'd offered it to him on a plate, only he'd nobly turned me down. And she believed him, of course.

But I didn't tell Dan, because I didn't have those discussions with my father. By the time I'd worked out what to say, Dan had stopped listening. He turned on the radio for *The Archers*. That stupid soap about a village full of middle-class farmers was the only thing Dan still had in common with Mum. He used to make me listen to it with him on that horrible holiday, just after he and Mum split up, when he was drunk all the time.

I went up to my room, my CDs. I really hate *The Archers*.

15

Aaron and I had the house to ourselves, and made full use of it. I was beginning to feel like a proper girlfriend. When we were at school, or e-mailing each other silly notes at night, our relationship felt like play-acting. On Aaron's bed, as we were getting all sweaty and excited, it was real.

One thing was still too real.

'You don't think I'm a slag, like Natasha?' I asked, after I'd been particularly nice to him. I was fishing for compliments, but, instead, I really set him off.

'I hate it when people call Nat a slag,' he said.

'There must be a reason they do that,' I murmured.

'Sure. These rumours started that she'd had an abortion and . . .' His voice trailed off.

'Were they true?' I asked. He didn't answer, so I went on. 'You're my boyfriend but you're really close to another girl. You've got to admit that's a bit weird.

Nobody'd blame me for being jealous, telling you to steer clear of her.'

'I'm not . . .' He looked away. I couldn't read his expression.

'I'm not asking you to walk away from a friend. Only, if you're going to be close to her, you've got to tell me what's happening. Otherwise I'm bound to fear the worst.'

Aaron thought for a moment. 'That's fair enough. But we're not as close as you think. I'm just the guy Natasha turns to when she's got nobody better to hang with.'

'Don't run yourself down,' I told him.

'I'm not. This weekend she . . . oh, it was all a big drama – how she'd seen the police and talked to Mrs Taylor.'

Mrs Taylor was the deputy head. 'Why her?' I asked.

'She's the "named person" at school, the one you're meant to go to if there's some kind of complaint against a teacher.'

'So Natasha went to her first?'

'No. She went to our form tutor. Mrs Gee told Nat that she wasn't allowed to keep it secret and arranged for Natasha to see Mrs Taylor. Anyhow, Natasha wanted to know what everyone was saying at school but I didn't know. I don't listen to gossip.'

'Did you tell her about me?' I asked, fishing again when I should have been finding out stuff for Dan.

'Nah. Natasha's not interested unless it affects her.'

'So she assumes you're at her beck and call. Remind me, why exactly are you her friend?'

Aaron's voice became more high-pitched as he got defensive. 'It's not like you're suggesting. I've known her forever. If I had a problem, she'd talk it through with me, advise me.'

'Done that before, has she?'

'I don't have serious problems.'

'Whereas I bet she has,' I said, showing my bitterness.

'Not recently. It's been months since we talked a lot.'

That made me feel better. Yet the paranoid part of me still suspected that Aaron and Natasha had concocted this whole thing. In my darkest moments, I even thought Aaron going out with me was part of some sick conspiracy against my dad. Aaron, naked beside me, seemed to sense how upset I was.

'I'd like to tell you everything,' he murmured. 'Only, I promised not to talk about it.'

'Natasha doesn't know you've got a girlfriend. You're not allowed to keep secrets from your girlfriend. It's wrong.'

'I don't want to keep secrets from you,' he assured me.

'If you don't trust me, how can I trust you?'

'Of course I trust you. And you can trust me. Really.'

'I want to trust you, more than anything. Don't you see I'm jealous . . .' I turned on the tears. It worked. He showed me what I needed to see.

16

I had a crush on a teacher once. It was early in Year Nine. He wasn't young – thirty or forty, I couldn't tell the difference – not even great looking. But Mr Finch dressed well, and he was single. And he was the only teacher who really noticed what was happening to me. He'd tell off girls who were teasing me, give little lectures about cooperation. He'd even force people to work with me when I was at my most skanky and gross.

I'm not sure Mr Finch ever knew that I liked him. It wasn't as though I talked much, to him or anyone else. Try as I did, more than once, I never managed to be alone in a room with him. I'd stick around with some dumb, fake question to ask and he'd walk me down the corridor, answering it as nicely as possible. If he was that careful with a Year Nine girl, how much more careful would he have been with a Year Eleven, especially one who looked like Natasha Clark?

* * *

Aaron's diary was in a folder on his PC, each file named after a month.

'How far back does it go?' I asked.

'I got this computer last summer holidays,' he explained. 'Before that, I had another one. Those diaries are saved on disk.' He opened September, then scrolled back page after page to the first week of the month.

'There,' he said. 'It's all on the screen.'

I read what was on screen without scrolling up or down, so couldn't see if he'd written anything about me. I guess not. It started just after he left the library with Natasha:

Went outside and walked her to the bus. She wouldn't talk. I kept at her and finally Nat told me Mr F had done something serious. Wouldn't say what, only pointed out the missing buttons on her shirt. I always avoid looking at her breasts, hadn't noticed the buttons had come off.

'He did that?'

'More than that,' she said, started crying. I held her, first time I've held her since the mess. Then I stroked her hair and she pulled away. My bad.

'You ought to tell someone,' I said. 'He shouldn't get away with stuff like that. He's a teacher.'

'But I let him,' she told me. 'I didn't say no even though I should've.'

'It makes no difference,' I said. 'Tell your mum.'

She stopped crying. 'Maybe I will. He deserves it.'

That was all. It hurt to read him being affectionate about another girl, one who'd suckered him completely. I felt like I knew less than I had before I read it. Why would Natasha make up a story like this? Why had Dan asked to see her? I read it a second time. I hated that phrase *my bad*. It came from some computer game. There was another phrase I didn't understand.

'What does this mean?' I asked. 'The mess?'

'When she got pregnant.'

'Oh.' I sensed it wasn't a good idea to ask about that. 'I don't know how you can remember all that conversation.'

Aaron laughed self-mockingly. 'I replay conversations in my head, all the time. I'm always going over what I said to see where I messed up.'

'I do that, too,' I admitted. 'Still, she doesn't exactly tell you what happened. Did he grope her? Try to attack her?'

'Nat told the teachers, and her mum, and the police. She didn't need to tell me.'

'But you're her friend.' And that's why she didn't tell you, I thought, because she couldn't lie so outrageously to you.

'And I'm still her friend. And you're my girlfriend. I'll tell her about you, I promise, now this is over for the moment.'

Over for the moment? What planet was he from? It was only just beginning. I wondered if Natasha knew that.

There was another thing I was even more curious about.

'Show me what you've written in your diary about me.'

'Can't do.'

'Go on . . .' I wheedled, reaching over for the mouse, I almost had the thing, but he whisked it away. I tried to grab it and we both started giggling.

'I want to see . . . please, pretty please. I won't tease you about whatever it says.'

'No!' Aaron closed down the computer.

'I'll be extra nice to you,' I offered.

'I'm not bargaining,' he said. 'I shouldn't have shown you what I just showed you. I've never shown anyone before. But I wanted you to know that I trusted you and you could trust me.'

He'd turned serious, so I did, too. 'I appreciate you showing me.'

'I don't write for an audience. If I thought that you were going to read my diary, it'd change the way I wrote about you – about everything, probably. It wouldn't be the same.'

'I understand. I was teasing, that's all. Forget it.'

I understood, all right. There were things in there he didn't want me to see, things I would kill to read. But he'd shown me that he trusted me. And I'd found out more about Natasha's allegations. I reckoned Aaron put the sex idea in her head. Then, unable to think of an allegation on the spot, she'd gone home and made one up.

Aaron walked me to the corner of my street, as usual. I figured that if he ever saw Dan's camper van parked there, he'd assume I didn't know who it belonged to. So far, he hadn't noticed and I hadn't had to lie. I hadn't lied to him once, unless you counted the little white lies about why I got the bus. I'd tell him the whole truth one day, after Dan was cleared and Aaron saw through Natasha.

When I got in, Dan was staring at the TV screen with

the sound on mute, mad-eyed. At least he wasn't drinking.

'My solicitor called,' he said. 'The police want me to go in tomorrow. I'm going to be charged with indecent assault.'

17

Mum drove me all the way home after my second weekend visit. Dan had called, saying that something had come up and he couldn't get back to the services in time so would she mind? Mum didn't mind. We hadn't had time to talk that weekend because Daisy had been ill.

'Has he got a girlfriend?' Mum asked, as the *Chart Show* finished and she turned the radio off.

'Not unless he only sees her alternate weekends.'

'I thought maybe that was where he was. You'd tell me if he was drinking again, wouldn't you?'

'Yes, but he's not.'

'Only I can't forget that time he took you on holiday and I had to come and collect you. When we picked you up, he absolutely stank and you looked so lost . . .'

'Dan's not back on the booze. He couldn't hold down a job if he was. And I wouldn't stay with him.'

Dan had a good excuse for drinking that summer.

His wife had left him for her boss. He had just as good a reason to drink now and he wasn't, hardly. But I couldn't tell Mum that.

'It wasn't just alcohol with your dad. He used to have this saying: *too much is, well, nowhere near enough*. Which was great when we were both students and everybody tried everything.'

'You tried everything?' I'd never even seen my mum drunk.

'I tried a few things I shouldn't have. Dan tried everything he could get his hands on.'

'I think he's grown out of that now.'

'As long as you'd tell me if . . .'

'I'd tell you,' I lied.

We were nearly there. 'Will you be all right in the house on your own?'

'I'll probably go to see Aaron.'

'I'd like to meet this boy some time,' Mum said, but didn't press it.

The house was cold. Dan had been away all weekend. I put on make-up, wrote a note saying I was at Aaron's, then hurried down the street while it was still light. Aaron would walk me home.

Only my boyfriend wasn't there. His sister said he was 'out'. His mum, who still wasn't sure what to make of me, came to the door. 'Did you try his mobile?'

'It's not on.' Aaron wasn't one of these people who are tied to their mobile, keeping it switched on all the time.

'Was he expecting you?'

'Kind of.'

'Here he is now,' Melanie called. A four-wheel drive was having difficulty negotiating the steep street. Sitting in the front seat was Natasha Clark. Aaron was in the back. As he got out, so did she. Natasha came over to me, ahead of Aaron. She was about my height and her clothes were nothing special, but she looked at least five years older than I felt.

'You must be Caitlin,' she said. 'Aaron's told me loads about you. I hope we're going to be friends.'

'Me too,' I mumbled.

As her father performed a six-point turn in the narrow road, Natasha leant forward conspiratorially. 'You're really lucky, you know. He's one in a million.'

'I know.'

She got back in and they drove off.

'My, you're popular with the ladies tonight,' Aaron's mum said, before we went up to his room.

'How is she?' I asked, when we were alone.

'She's OK. The police have charged Mr Fordham,

which means they're sure he did it. That's good, Nat reckons. She was worried because the police warned her the majority of cases like this one never go to court. It'll still be a couple of months.'

I'd been doing some searching on the internet, and knew that cases like this took more like nine months to get to court. In the end, only a tiny percentage of teachers were ever found guilty. But I didn't mention this. Instead I said, 'What I don't understand is how they'll be able to prove it, either way – surely it's her word against his?'

'Yeah. I know. But Nat reckons they've got a witness, somebody who saw some of what happened.'

This was news to me. I was sure it would be news to Dan too. 'Who? Not you?'

'No, I was in the library with you, stupid.'

'Don't call me stupid!' I tickled him. I'd been worried that Aaron might be willing to lie for Natasha. I was relieved the witness wasn't him. But who was it?

Aaron tickled me back. It led to other things. We only got round to talking about Natasha again when he walked me home.

'I'm glad you two met today. I've told her all about you and she wants to get to know you. She figured it wasn't a good situation, me being the only person you see outside school.'

This might be true. Holly had invited me round a couple of times but I'd ducked out (easily done, since she lived on the other side of the city). Yet I could so not see Natasha getting friendly with a girl in the year below her. Patronising cow.

'That'd be nice,' I said. We were on my road.

'Want me to see you to the door?'

I was about to say 'yes' when I saw the camper van was back.

'You're all right,' I said, giving him a big, wet, sloppy kiss. 'In fact, you're more than all right.'

'I love you,' he said, and I was so shocked I said nothing back, just watched him walk round the corner, out of sight, before I went in to ask my dad where the hell he'd been.

18

A few days later, I borrowed the transcripts of Dan's police interviews from his desk (the police had to give his solicitor a copy of the tape, which was then transcribed). On the tape, the police kept asking the same questions in different ways, which was a waste of time: Dan could be impulsive, but he was never stupid. I read and reread the transcript to get a clearer picture of what had happened.

Why did you ask to see Natasha that afternoon?

I didn't ask to see her. She came to see me.

Do you often see young women on their own after school?

No. I rarely give detentions. If I do, I generally keep more than one child behind, so it's less wasteful of my time.

Yet you arranged to see Natasha Clark on her own.

No, she turned up out of the blue at the end of the day.

Earlier, you said that it was an appointment.

I'm not aware of giving any such impression.

Members of her class say you talked privately to Natasha in that day's lesson, as though setting a time for a meeting.

No. That's definitely not the case.

What did you discuss with her during the lesson?

I don't recall.

When she turned up 'out of the blue', what did she give as a reason?

She had an overdue piece of coursework and wanted me to look it over before I took it in, make sure she was on the right lines. Once a piece has been handed in, you can't rewrite it.

Was that unusual?

Yes, a little. Possibly I'd nagged her about it in the lesson, I don't recall.

So you saw her on your own?

She turned up just after my last class had left. I was tired at the end of the day. It wasn't a situation which concerned me. I'd taught Natasha for a year without any problems. She wanted me to give her assignment a quick once-over, or so she said. But, while I was reading . . .

Go on.

She leant over and I saw that she'd undone a button or two of her school shirt, was practically falling out of it.

And she's a well-endowed young lady, isn't she?

Naturally, my alarm bells went off.

But you didn't leave immediately. You must have heard the stories about her.

An attractive girl at that age comes under all kinds of pressure. Often they're labelled as either frigid or promiscuous – it's one of the issues we teach in Social Education. I thought I could deal with the situation.

And what did you do?

I stood up and tried to bring the meeting to an end. Possibly I told her to leave the assignment with me.

And did she?

Not that I recall.

Do you recall what the assignment was about?

The language of newspapers, I think.

According to the girl, there was no assignment. You asked to see her about improving her grades.

That's . . . rubbish. I mean, that's . . .

The oldest line in the teacher's book, yes. Perhaps you'd like to tell us what happened next. You stood up . . .

She stood, too. I thought she was going to leave and I still had things to clear up, so I didn't move. In retrospect, I should have walked straight out because then she said she felt faint. I reached out to support her. And then she kissed me.

You're much taller than her. Did she have trouble reaching?

Not as I recall. She may have stood on tiptoe. It all happened very quickly.

It was a quick kiss, a sort of sneak attack?

No. Yes. I mean, I don't know how I'd characterise it.

Did you enjoy it?

God, no. I've got a daughter that age! Do you think I'm . . .? She tried to put her tongue down my throat. I pushed her away.

But not before she'd put her tongue down your throat? Where were her hands?

I'm not sure. We're talking seconds here, fractions of seconds. Picture it. It's the end of the day. I'm tired. A girl comes in and throws herself at me. It's not a common situation and I think I handled it responsibly.

Yet you didn't report it to her form teacher, or her Head of Year. Why not?

I should have done, obviously. I meant to mention it to somebody. But before I could . . .

(a long pause at this point.)

You were seen, you know.

Pardon?

The curtains weren't closed and the door was unlocked. Taking quite a risk.

I had nothing to hide. You say someone saw what happened? Then they can tell you I did nothing wrong.

Now that you know there was a witness, I'm going to give you another chance to get your story straight. Those two buttons of Natasha's which were undone - you did that, didn't you? The kiss, that was your move too? Natasha was so shocked that she let you kiss her, then tried to pull away when you put your tongue in her mouth and groped her breasts, popping open two of her buttons. Come on, man. You were seen!

Anyone who says they saw that is a malicious liar. I let the girl kiss me for a moment or two. I did not grope her.

You then held onto her and made graphic sexual suggestions which upset her. At which point, she started to shout, so you let her go. She was heard, Mr Fordham.

She said . . . something, I can't remember exactly. Something about my regretting turning her down. That's all, I swear.

No need to swear now. You can do that in court.

19

Our side of the city shimmered under the hard, bright October sun. October was my favourite time of year, just before the leaves fall and winter sets in. Last year, good days were few and far between. Clouds covered the sky. This year, the weather was fine but for one, constant, ominous cloud.

Dan had taken to long walks and reading the Russians. Each doorstopper paperback would last him a week: Tolstoy, Dostoevsky, Pushkin. And the doctor had put him on tranquillisers.

When I mentioned the witness, he had no idea who it was.

'Unless it's someone who's been put up to it by Natasha, they couldn't have seen anything incriminating,' he insisted.

One day, when I got home from school, I found he'd had a haircut, even done the washing and ironing.

'We've got company for dinner tomorrow.'

'Who?'

'A friend who's coming for the weekend. You can invite someone if you want.'

'There's only Aaron.'

Dan looked awkward. He knew I was seeing Aaron but we never discussed my having a boyfriend.

'I guess . . .'

'And he doesn't know who you are.'

Dan thought aloud. 'I suppose he can keep a secret.'

'I don't want him to have to keep secrets. Anyhow, it's more complicated than that. He's friendly with Natasha. They've known each other since Infants.'

That was the last time Dan mentioned inviting Aaron over.

Dan's weekend guest was Jo Grant. It was her he'd been to see three weeks earlier when he was late back on the Sunday night. She looked older and thinner than when we'd met six months earlier. Maybe teaching does that. She'd also split up with her university boyfriend: for good this time, or so she said.

Jo was keen to let me know that she wasn't getting back together with my dad.

'But I'm here for him. And for you, too. This must be a heavy time.'

'Pretty heavy,' I mumbled.

'Dan tells me you've got a boyfriend now. I remember Aaron. He's a really nice lad. If there's anything you want to talk about, just between us, stuff you can't ask your mum . . .'

'Thanks. I'm fairly sorted.' If Jo thought I was going to discuss sex stuff with her, she had another think coming. She might gross me out by talking about things she used to do with my dad. Neither Dan nor Aaron knew that I was taking the pill (I didn't exactly hide them, but Dan hardly ever came in my room). Aaron and I never talked about what we did on his single bed. I could tell Aaron why I was on the pill, but he might assume I was a slag, the way those bitches at my old school did. He might put pressure on me to have sex straight away. I meant to do it with him, but only when it felt right, or as right as it was ever going to feel.

Turned out Dan had written to Jo, telling her what was happening and saying that, as she was the last person he'd had a relationship with, he might need her as a character witness. Jo, who'd just been chucked, had come running to see him.

Later, when I was trying to sleep, I could clearly hear the two of them across the landing, shagging each other's brains out. So much for her not getting back together with him. I couldn't sleep. To block them out, I put music on the headphones and wrote Aaron a long e-mail telling him how much I loved him. Funny, while I could never say it to his face, writing it down was easy.

I felt my heart slip through my hands as I pressed 'send'.

20

'Your father's girlfriend . . .' Trevor was driving me all the way back because Dan was staying with Jo. The 'meet halfway' routine had lasted precisely two weekends. 'What's she like?'

'Jo? Like Kate Moss, only younger, with shorter hair.'

That shut him up. I'd seen Trevor looking at photos of Kate Moss, always 'tastefully' nude, advertising some cologne. She even looked fantastic straight after she had a baby. Mum, meanwhile, had never lost the fat she put on round the middle when she was pregnant with Daisy. Trevor might have stolen Mum, but now he thought Dan was having it away with his favourite fantasy. That would mess with his head.

Mum had been preoccupied most of the weekend, only half there. There was a moment, though, when she tried to talk to me about Dan. Three years on, and she was still apologising for leaving him.

'I know he's your father and you want to think

he's a good man. He is a good man. Only . . .' For a moment, I thought she'd found out. I was ready to leap to his defence. But then she saw the way I was looking at her and backed off.

'OK, I won't go there. Just as long as you know you can always . . .' Her expression said the rest. I let my silence speak. I knew more than she did.

Trevor dropped me at Aaron's, as prearranged. The Sunday train connections were crap. Dan wasn't coming back from Jo's until Monday (though neither Trevor nor Janet knew this). Aaron would walk me home later. I said 'thanks' to Trevor and was about to ring the doorbell when Janet came out. She waved at Trevor, who wound down the window on his people carrier.

'You must be Caitlin's father.'

'Stepfather. Trevor Millingham. I've heard a lot about your son, but we haven't had the pleasure of meeting him yet.'

'Aaron! Get out here for a minute!'

A bashful Aaron appeared. I cowered in embarrassment. Aaron shook Trevor's hand.

'You must come over and stay with us in Derbyshire one weekend, Aaron. That is, if your mother's happy for you to.'

'If there were certain ground rules . . .' said Janet, clearly impressed by Trevor's posh car and posh voice.

'Of course. It's a big house. Plenty of room for guests. And Sheila would love to meet Aaron.'

What was Janet worrying about anyhow? It's the girls' parents who have to look out for casual pregnancies. Boys are expected to sow wild oats.

After oiling around Aaron and Janet for endless minutes, Trevor set off back to Parwich. I was allowed up to Aaron's room. But I could never completely relax when Janet was home. She might appear at the door at any minute with coffee and shortbread or a phone message she'd forgotten earlier.

'Want to come back to mine?' I suggested to Aaron.

'Won't your dad . . . ?'

'He's not coming back 'til tomorrow. Train problems. I thought you could walk me home then phone your mum and say my dad's been delayed, so you're going to stay 'til he gets home.'

'Brilliant idea.'

I thought it was brilliant, too, because it meant that I finally got to take Aaron home without any risk of him meeting Dan. It didn't occur to me until we were halfway there that Aaron would see this as a god-given opportunity for us to finally have full sex.

21

Afterwards, as he dressed, Aaron looked out of the window.

'Whose is that camper van?'

My heart sank. 'Somebody down the street.'

'Mr Fordham's got one like that. It's not him, is it?'

'The teacher? I don't know what he looks like. He was suspended just after I arrived.'

'I wonder what's happening with that,' Aaron said.

'Doesn't Natasha tell you?'

'She's got a new boyfriend. I think she's over it now.'

Over it! Dan still had months to go before the whole thing went to trial. I acted as though I'd just remembered something.

'Didn't you say there was a witness?'

'That's what Nat said.'

'Who is it? A friend of Natasha's?'

'She didn't tell me who. I got the impression it was

somebody she didn't know. Listen, it's nearly midnight. My mum'll have a fit if I don't get back soon.'

'She'll be asleep, won't she?'

'You don't know my mum. I'll phone now. Tell her your dad's train only just got in.'

'OK.'

He used the house phone, rather than his mobile. I looked around one more time, making sure there was nothing to give away Dan's identity. If Aaron found out I'd lied to him the very night we first did it, how would he feel about me? Maybe, after Dan was found not guilty, he'd be OK with my dad being Mr Fordham. But I doubted it.

After Aaron left, I didn't sleep for ages, going over everything that had happened. It wasn't the sex that mattered most – the act was awkward and over before I'd managed to start enjoying it – but the closeness, the knowing that I was Aaron's first lover. I was glad we'd done it, even though I felt a bit rushed. I was glad we'd got it over with. Next time was bound to be better.

In the morning, I had a lie in. Dan would be back at lunchtime. He could give me a lift to school then, if he insisted.

It had gone eleven when the doorbell rang. I was dressed, just, but nearly didn't answer it, not expecting anybody. Suppose it was Aaron and he'd taken the day off, too?

The bloke in the doorway was Dan's age or older, with a hangdog face and thick, grey hair. He was surprised to see me.

'Does Dan Fordham live here?'

'Who wants to know?' I thought he was another reporter.

'My name's John. Dan's expecting me. Barry at the union asked . . .'

'Dan's in London, visiting his girlfriend. I'm expecting him back soon.'

'I guess I'm a little early.'

I explained who I was, claiming to have the morning off school. I wasn't wearing my uniform. Let him think I was a sixth former. That morning, I felt like a sixth former. John looked embarrassed.

'You may as well come in,' I said.

'Better not,' he said, in his shambling, vulnerable way. 'I can come back a bit later.'

'Up to you. But I'm not sure exactly when he'll be back.'

Dan wasn't the world's most reliable timekeeper. The

sky opened, as it had been threatening to all morning.

'Come on,' I said, and John scurried inside.

While I made him a cup of tea, John established that I knew what was going on with Dan.

'How's he holding up?'

'Pretty crap. He's just got back together with his old girlfriend though. I think that's helping.'

'He's lucky. In circumstances like these, most people assume you're guilty, treat you like a pariah.'

He sounded like he'd been through it himself. I passed him his tea. 'Are you going to tell me why you're here?'

'The union tries to put suspended teachers in touch with others who've been through the same process. It can be very lonely, very stressful.'

'You were accused of the same thing?'

John nodded. 'I used to be a primary school teacher. I was always very careful about how I handled myself – left doors open, didn't keep children behind on their own, the stuff they drum into you during teacher training. Then I was accused of feeling up a nine-year-old.'

He looked at me for signs of shock, but not much shocked or surprised me any more, and I wouldn't have shown him if it had.

'I was supposed to have done this several times, while there was a full class of kids with me at the time. The story was absurd. But I was suspended straight away. The police looked at the classroom where I worked. They said the allegations didn't make sense. After a few weeks, they dropped the case. But I was still suspended. And before there was a local authority hearing to let me back into the classroom, the police arrested me again. Wild gossip in the playground. Another kid said I'd done something. Everybody turned against me. If my wife hadn't stood by me . . .'

John's voice tailed off. He was clearly used to telling his story, yet it still affected him.

'There were ten months before it went to trial. The jury took twenty minutes to find me not guilty. But, by then, I hadn't had a full night's sleep for a year. I'd lost weight. There was no way I'd ever go back into the classroom, anywhere.'

'Why did they do it?' I asked. 'Make up lies about you?'

'Don't go looking for reasons,' John said. 'That way, madness lies. It's a fucked-up world, out there – excuse my language.'

'You think it'll help my dad for you to tell him all this?'

'To meet somebody else who's been through it helps, so they say. There are pitfalls he can avoid. Has the named contact person from school been in touch, for instance?'

'I don't think so.'

'That's important. They . . .'

There was the sound of a key in the lock.

'It'd probably be best if I talked to your dad on his own.'

'Of course.'

'Cate? What are you . . . ?' Dan stopped when he saw John. There was a brief look of panic in his eyes, as though John might have come to take Dan – or me – away. I explained who he was, adding: 'I took the morning off but I'm about to get the bus in.'

I took my time getting changed. When I came back down, in my school uniform, Dan and John were deep in conversation. As I pushed the door open, I overheard their conversation.

'I could never go back into teaching. I do scut work while I try to decide what to do next. My confidence is coming back, slowly. Talking to people like you helps, in an odd way. Helping other teachers not to go through as much hell as I did.'

Dan looked embarrassed. 'It must be worse when

it's primary school kids – the whole paedophile thing.'

'Underage girls is bad enough. They have very vivid—'

'Are you off, Cate?' Dan interrupted. 'Sorry I can't give you a lift.'

'It's all right. I should get there by the end of lunch.'

John stood up and shook hands with me. 'You've got a very mature daughter there,' he told Dan. 'She must be a source of strength to you.'

'She is,' Dan said. 'See you later, love.'

'Love' was a standard greeting in Sheffield, but Dan never used it. I smiled awkwardly before saying 'goodbye'. Nobody had ever called me 'mature' before, either. I wondered if it was true.

22

Two summers ago, back when I was an acne-scarred, multiply-pierced, chain-smoking, black-wearing thirteen-year-old, I stole Trevor's car and drove it from Parwich to Bakewell. It was a terrifying journey, but I wanted to meet this guy I'd 'connected' with in a chat room. I thought my turning up in the car would convince him I was seventeen. Only it turned out he'd lied to me about his age just as I'd lied to him about mine. He was only fifteen. When his mother saw some girl show up in a car she obviously wasn't old enough to drive, she called the police.

Trevor kept at me about how on earth I'd learned to drive, so I said: 'D'oh! Anybody can drive an automatic.' Which is true, especially if your father taught you to operate the stick shift in a VW camper van as soon as you were tall enough to reach the pedals. I could have blamed this escapade on Dan – it's so easy to blame everything on your parents:

after all, without them, you wouldn't even be alive. At the time, I hadn't seen Dan for eighteen months. I was busy rebuilding him in this idealised image, fantasising about what it would be like if I lived with him instead of Trevor and my newly-pregnant Mum.

Over the last few weeks, there'd been so much going on, I hadn't got round to becoming the new person I'd meant to be in Sheffield: the positive, popular(ish) daddy's girl, with a select bunch of friends. At school, I kept everyone except Aaron at a distance. At least having a boyfriend in Year Eleven meant I got a fair amount of respect. I was the same person I was at school in Derbyshire but I was treated totally differently. Appearance and reputation are what people judge you on – not what you're really like.

Natasha's reputation was about as suspect as you could get. Since Dan got suspended, every kid in Year Seven had heard the history of her sexual life. Dan was still popular. Kids resented having a supply teacher instead of him. There were some who, when Natasha passed near them, made hissing noises.

Did I feel sorry for her? No way. But I couldn't

gloat either. I wanted to hate her but, to really hate somebody, you have to know them, and that wasn't likely to happen.

Then a weird thing happened. I was on my way to Maths when I saw Natasha cruising along the corridor with a bunch of her cronies. Natasha stopped, leaving the others to walk on.

'Hi, Caitlin. How's it going?'

Too numb to react properly, I mumbled something and kept walking.

Trouble was, from then on, Natasha said 'hello' every time we passed each other in the corridor. At first, I scuttled off. But, however much I hated her, I couldn't treat her as my enemy, not when Aaron was still friendly with her. I half expected him to mention how I was ignoring his oldest mate. I didn't know how I'd reply if he did.

At afternoon registrations, Holly asked me what I was doing at the weekend. I mumbled something about being busy.

'You'll be seeing Aaron, I guess.'

'He only lives down the road, so it's pretty likely.'

'Don't get a strop on,' Holly said. 'We haven't all got boyfriends.'

'I know. Sorry.' I should have said something

friendly. Since getting off with Aaron I hardly spoke to Holly. It made far more sense for me to hang out with her than with Natasha. Yet that's what I began to do.

About a week after that first 'How's it going?' I was smoking behind the trees at the edge of the playing fields. Natasha joined me.

'Bet Aaron doesn't know you smoke. Give us a drag.'

I passed it to her. 'How do you stand it?' I asked.

'What?'

'You know, the hissing, the gossip, the way all those morons look at you.'

'I don't mind the kids,' Natasha told me. 'They're too young to know better. It's the teachers . . .'

'The teachers?'

'Yeah. The poison in some of their eyes. They keep their distance. If someone makes a crack about Fordham and me, it's like we're not allowed to go there but every last bit of their body language says *it's all that lying little bitch's fault.*'

'Why do you take it?' I asked, as Natasha handed the cigarette back.

'What am I supposed to do – change schools in my last year and muck up my GCSEs? No thanks.'

'You must have known all this would happen when you accused Mr Fordham . . .'

Natasha shook her head, took the cigarette back and sucked it down to the filter. 'Didn't cross my mind.'

'Did Aaron talk you into it – reporting him, I mean?'

Natasha gave me a wary, half-amused look. 'He's your boyfriend. Ask him.'

'He says you didn't tell him much.'

'Aaron's a nice guy. I like to protect him.'

I wondered what she meant by this. Natasha finished my cigarette and stubbed it out on the patchy grass. I asked the question that my dad would really like answered.

'Aaron says somebody else saw what happened.'

'Yeah. One of the staff. Dunno how much he saw, but enough to satisfy the police.'

'You don't know who it was?'

'Who cares?' Natasha was starting to sound tetchy. 'Why are you so interested?'

I went sullen on her. 'Just making conversation.'

Natasha seemed to accept this. 'Sorry, I get pissed off with people trying to pump me for information about Fordham. Like I want to talk about that crap.'

'Let's change the subject, then. Aaron says you've got a new boyfriend.'

'Had. A trainee nurse called Tim. He seemed really sensitive – you know the act. Took me the best part of a fortnight to work out he just wanted to use me for sex.'

I should have acted like I felt sorry for her. But I couldn't. 'Are you sure you weren't using him for sex, too?'

Natasha got out a pack of Marlboro Lights and offered me one. There wasn't time before break ended but I lit up anyway.

'He didn't get any. Sex isn't high on my list of priorities.'

'But you've had lots of blokes.'

Natasha shook her head. 'Lots of boyfriends. I only slept with two. And I thought I was in love with both of them.'

I was taken aback. 'But they weren't in love with you?'

Natasha shrugged. 'Love's the excuse guys use to get into your knickers. Aaron's the only one who treats me like a person, who likes me for myself. So you're really lucky.'

Natasha stubbed out her half-smoked cigarette and

left for her lesson. I cursed out loud, having realised what I should have guessed from the start: Aaron was not only Natasha's closest friend, he was also the love of her life. One day, she'd realise it. In the meantime, he was playing a long game: hoping, expecting, to get her in the end. Me, he was just using.

23

Janet let me wait in Aaron's room. 'He's seeing a friend. Was he expecting you?'

'I don't think I said a precise time,' I lied. 'Guess I must be early.'

'Is everything all right?' Aaron's mum asked.

'I needed to get out of the house. My dad's got girlfriend trouble. He's really on edge.'

This made Janet curious. She was interested in my dad, probably because they'd never met. I kept very vague about him, so Janet might imagine him as someone mature and eligible.

'Have they been together long?'

'Just under a year, off and on. More off than on.'

'I'll give Aaron a call, tell him you're here.'

'Whatever. Give him a few minutes. I don't want to seem like I'm . . . I dunno, possessive of his time or something.'

'That's sensible,' Janet said. 'At your age, if you

don't mind me saying, it's easy to go overboard in all sorts of ways.'

'Aaron's my first boyfriend. I don't want to blow it.'

This seemed to reassure her. As soon as she was gone, I turned on Aaron's PC, connected to the internet and loaded a site as cover. Then I opened up Outlook Express. As I suspected, there were a whole bunch of e-mails from Natasha. I didn't have time to read them. I thought of forwarding them all to myself, but that would have left a record, one of those green arrow symbols. So I opened several then cut and pasted the contents into a big e-mail which I addressed to myself.

I was about to hit 'send' when I had another idea. I took a deep breath and clicked on 'add attachment'. Up came a list of what was on Aaron's desktop. I highlighted the folder in which he stored his diaries and clicked on 'choose' for the most recent file. That was safer than opening the diaries and reading them then. If he suspected me of doing that, all he had to do was check when the file had last been modified. Since Janet never went near his computer, he'd know it was me.

I selected the files for September and October. I would have gone for the whole lot but Aaron might be home any second.

By the time I pressed 'send', I'd been in Aaron's room for ten minutes. It was quarter past eight. I'd told Aaron I'd be round by half past. I knew where he was, at Natasha's. But Aaron was reliable. He would be home any moment. The attachment seemed to be taking forever to send. How big were those files?

Too late. Downstairs, I heard a door slam. He was home. I had less than a minute. There had to be a way of cancelling the e-mail, aborting the whole message, but I'd never used it and didn't know how. I had to find it now. Aaron paused on the landing to answer a question from Janet. Then I heard his footsteps again. The computer made the sudden ker-ching noise which meant the message has gone. Now I had to move fast, really fast. I went to the 'sent items' folder and deleted the e-mail I'd just sent. Then I went to the 'deleted items' folder and deleted it again. As the door opened, I quit Outlook Express.

'What are you doing?' Aaron asked.

'I got here early so I was catching up on some blogs.'

Aaron looked at the Internet Explorer display on the desktop and seemed satisfied. 'Found any good ones?'

I showed him Neil Gaiman's web-log, which I'd picked because I knew that Aaron was a huge *Sandman* fan. He read a few paragraphs then bookmarked it.

'Where've you been? Natasha's?'

'Yeah. I went round for my tea. She said she'd spent some time with you the other day. I'm glad you two are cool.'

He came over and began to feel me up. I stopped him after a couple of minutes. 'Not with your mum downstairs.'

'She won't come up. She likes you now. Everything's fine.'

'Even so . . .' I wanted to get home and read the e-mail I'd just sent myself. We'd had sex in his room twice. Both times, Janet and Melanie were out, but I was still nervous, worried Janet would burst in on us like the first time I'd met her.

'I promised Dad I'd get home in time to watch this show with him,' I said. It was half true. Dan liked it when we watched things together and discussed them afterwards.

'But you only just got here.'

'I came early. I didn't know you were going to Natasha's.'

Aaron said nothing. For she would always come first. We both knew that.

24

Next morning, Dan was in a state.

'She hasn't called all week. I've left messages and texted her . . . nothing.'

'Go and see her.' I felt guilty. I'd pretended to Janet that Jo had dumped Dan. Now it looked like she had.

'I don't like leaving you.'

'I'm fifteen next week. It's not against the law to leave me on my own. Stay overnight if it works out.'

'All right. If I catch the midday train, I'll get there in time to meet her from school. Whatever happens, I'll be on the last train back. I'm seeing my solicitor at ten tomorrow.'

As soon as I got home that night, I checked my e-mail (I had my own computer in Parwich, but shared Dan's in Sheffield. He couldn't get at my e-mail, though, because I used an account you could only access with a password). Hotmail was down: a message told me to try later. I read some of my favourite blogs to pass the time, but the server was still down when I tried again. As soon as I disconnected, the phone rang. Aaron.

'Did you get the e-mail I sent after you left last night?'

For a moment, I panicked. Had he worked out what I'd done?

'No.' I explained why not.

'You should never rely on anything that's free,' Aaron said. Then he began to tell me about his e-mail, which was a list of different ways I might like to spend my birthday.

'I'll have to consider that,' I said. 'But I can think of what I'd like to do with you right now. Dad's out all evening.'

Aaron chuckled. 'I'll be over as soon as I've had my tea.'

I was sorry I'd left in a huff the night before. So I showered and put on a little make-up. Then I went round the house removing anything with Dan's name on it. There were no photos of him. Dan wasn't vain that way. There was one of me with Jo, which I hid. Aaron might wonder how I knew her.

When Aaron arrived, we went straight to bed. I wanted to escape into his arms. Yet, as we were doing it, my mind began to wander. What was in all those e-mails that Natasha sent him? Would I be able to open the attachment holding his diary?

'Still! I thought I heard something . . .'

Aaron stopped. I listened. This area was notorious for burglars. Dan kept a baseball bat under his bed in case one broke in during the night.

'You're right,' Aaron said. 'Footsteps.'

I began to pull myself off Aaron. Too late. The door flew open.

'Cate . . . Jesus Christ!'

'Get out! GET OUT!' I screeched.

Dan did. Had Aaron seen him? My boyfriend was putting on his clothes.

'I thought he was out until late.'

'So did I,' I said, tugging on underwear.

I stared at him, panicking. No sign of anything but embarrassment. If Aaron had recognised Dan . . . but no, if I was in Aaron's position, I wouldn't have looked at my father's face either. As long as Dan stayed out of the way until Aaron was gone . . . I ushered Aaron down the stairs. In the living room, I could hear my father crying.

'Oh shit, oh shit,' Aaron said, beneath his breath.

'It'll be OK,' I told Aaron at the door. 'I love you.'

'Love you too.' He hurried out, passing Dan's camper van.

Dan didn't look at me. He'd been crying.

'She's gone back to him.'

'I'm sorry.'

Dan had stopped at the off-licence on the way back from the station. There were two bottles of vodka on the table, one of them opened. He was drinking it neat.

I waited for a moment in case there was a lecture, but he said nothing. I kissed him on the forehead, the way he kissed me, then climbed the steep stairs back to my room.

I waited for Dan to go to bed so that I could go downstairs and use the computer. But he was still awake at two, drinking and smoking and listening to maudlin music by The Smiths and Nick Cave.

When I went down in the morning I saw that he'd made a start on the second bottle of vodka. Before leaving for school, I left a note reminding him about his meeting at ten.

25

That evening, Dan was tight-lipped about his meeting with the solicitor.

'Nothing to report. No sign of a court date. It could drag on and on. Here.'

Without looking at me, he pushed a leaflet from the local family planning clinic across the table. There was a big circle around the section where it said all appointments were confidential and gave the phone number. I looked at it politely then pushed the thing back to him.

'Mum put me on the pill. For my skin. It's OK.'

On the drive to Parwich, Dan was, for once, at a loss for words. He dropped me outside the cottage and drove off without speaking to Mum.

'You're looking really good, Cate,' Trevor told me. 'Changed your hair?'

'No.' My hair had grown out and looked more

natural, the way Aaron liked it. But that wasn't what Trevor was admiring. He was seeing the glow that came from me being in love with Aaron.

As soon as I could, I made my excuses and went upstairs to use the internet. When I logged on, there were three messages from Aaron – one about the other night, another about birthday ideas. Then I got to the one that appeared to be from him, but wasn't: the one I'd sent myself, with three months of his diary attached.

There was less in Natasha's e-mails than I'd hoped, or feared. The earliest one was from the summer holidays and titled 're: Wednesday.'

Supposed to be seeing bf tomorrow but if it doesn't pan out I'll txt u.
  Thanks for the offer.
  xN

The kiss meant nothing. Lots of people used them. I didn't know which boyfriend 'bf' referred to, or what Aaron had written in the first place. Natasha wasn't one of those people who left the old e-mail underneath their reply. What had Aaron suggested? A visit or a movie . . . who cared? I did. We hardly ever went on dates which involved us spending money. Though at least he was offering to take me somewhere for my birthday.

I'd gone through his e-mails as far back as August, but I hadn't pasted in the dates, which made for a confusing read. There were another couple of nothingy ones, turning down suggested meetings, and one which said 'good to see you the other day'. It sounded like Aaron had gone round there on the off chance of finding her in, got lucky. Then there was one which seemed to have been sent after she made the allegation.

Laying low for a week until things calm down. Come and see me tomorrow. I want to hear what they're all saying. Is DF still in school?
xxNat

'DF' suggested she knew my dad's first name, though that meant little. Dan was the sort of teacher who'd tell kids to 'call me Dan' even though it was against school policy.

I read the remaining e-mails quickly, as Mum was calling me for dinner. They were about meeting up. No secrets, except that Aaron had been seeing her out of school more often than he told me. Finally, while I was still on-line, I tried to open the first attachment. My heartbeat raced as a window appeared, saying that no viruses had been found.

'Caitlin! We're waiting.'

'Coming.'

I downloaded the most recent file. Words filled the screen. I scrolled down. There was page of page of them. Feeling like a thief, I downloaded September, then October, putting each file into a folder marked 'coursework'. Mum gave up shouting.

When I got downstairs, they were already eating. I could see that Mum was fuming, but Trevor was in peacekeeper mode. He even offered me a glass of wine with my main course. I shook my head and snapped at him.

'You shouldn't give booze to fourteen-year-old girls.'

'You're fifteen next weekend. We're happy for you to learn to drink a little, responsibly. Better that than—'

I didn't let him finish. 'Well, you needn't worry because I'm never going to drink, ever!'

Mum smiled knowingly, that really irritating look she has which I've noticed myself use, making me hate myself even more.

'In that case, all we have to do is wean you off the cigarettes. I cleared six stubs from outside your window last time you were here.'

'Maybe I'll give up tobacco and smoke weed instead,' I offered. 'It's safer.'

'If I catch you with any, or hear of you using it, you're grounded for six months.'

Mum meant it. I was grounded for most of Year Nine. But the threat was nearly meaningless now I lived with Dan. Also, I had no friends in Parwich to go out with – or get weed from. Trevor, anxious to clear the air, filled me in on the state of the campaign to save the village shop.

That night, after I was supposed to have gone to bed, my door opened.

'Cate. Are you still up? Oh, you're on the internet. Have you been crying?' Mum came over and hugged me. 'What is it? Aren't things working out with your dad?'

'It's not that,' I said. 'Boyfriend problems.'

'But you said that everything with Aaron was fine. We were thinking of inviting him over at Christmas.'

'He's just using me as a stopgap,' I told her. 'He

doesn't really love me. He's in love with somebody else.'

'I doubt that that's true,' Mum told me, wiping my eyes with a tissue she had tucked in her sleeve. 'You're both too young to be sure about your feelings. I expect you're imagining it.'

But I knew I wasn't. I had, after all, just read his diary.

26

Aaron loved to write. I already knew that from his e-mails. Some days, he'd written over a thousand words in his journal. I felt guilty about reading my boyfriend's diary. I wanted to gulp it all down, get it over with. Rather than read the whole thing, I decided to do a word search, skipping to the sections which mentioned Natasha, Dan or me. I'd like to say that what follows is all I read, that I took what I needed to take and left Aaron some privacy. But I went on to read every last word, more than once.

I was in love with him. I wanted to get inside his head. Does that make me a bad person?

AUGUST

Went to see Nat but she was out. Pat told me she's hardly been home this summer hols, then: 'but you know all about that', as if Nat's been with me. So I waited for her to come home in case she was using me as an alibi. Ten when she showed. I was by the bus stop, but she came from the other end of the street, wearing high heels. Knew better than to ask who'd given her a lift. We talked about sweet f a for a few minutes, then she thanked me for waiting around, said why don't we go to a movie or something before term starts. Acted a little drunk, though I couldn't smell booze on her. Maybe she was high on something else. I ought to be happy she's happy. But I'm not. I ought to leave her be. I won't.

SEPTEMBER

First day back. Nat in funny mood, snappy sullen. Tried to talk to her at break but she disappeared. Started smoking again? She ate her lunch with me, said sorry for hardly seeing me all summer. She'd make it up to me. I suggested we meet later but N said she had some things to sort out. Then told me I really ought to get a girlfriend. Hah, fucking hah.

Talked to Nat in English – she hadn't finished the Maths h/w. Offered to help her after school. Didn't want me to go round hers. Said meet in the library, which was weird. She doesn't use libraries. N wasn't there when I showed up only – serendipity – this other girl was. New in Year Ten. Long straight dark hair, pale skin like some Disney princess. Kept looking at her over my paper. Finally she spoke to me. We swapped papers and introduced ourselves. Kate. Posh voice, but not stuck up. Turns out she lives near me. I thought, Natasha set this up! She told Kate to be here so she could meet me. But no, if Nat was going to set me up, she'd have done it ages ago. Also, this girl's new, hasn't had time to meet Nat.

I was working up the nerve to ask her out when Nat walked in, looking like someone had stuffed shit in her mouth.

Went outside and walked her to the bus. She wouldn't talk. I kept at her and finally Nat told me Mr F had done something serious. Wouldn't say what, only pointed out the missing buttons on her shirt. I always avoid looking at her breasts, hadn't noticed they were missing.

'He did that?'

'More than that,' she said, started crying. I held her, first time I've held her since the mess. Then I stroked her hair and she pulled away. My bad.

'You ought to tell someone,' I said. 'He shouldn't get away with stuff like that. He's a teacher.'

'But I let him,' she told me. 'I didn't say no even though I should've.'

'It makes no difference,' I said. 'Tell your mum.'

She stopped crying. 'Maybe I will. He deserves it.'

Insisted on going back with her. When we got in, Nat rushed upstairs. Told Pat what I thought happened. Pat went ballistic. When she calmed down, she gave me a fiver for a taxi home. Walked home, thinking about Fordham. He's always had an eye for Nat. When I said so last year people said I was jealous. Fordham didn't look at Nat any more than anybody else. You can't blame a teacher for looking at a fit girl plus everybody knew he was going out with Ms Grant. I figured they were right. I was imagining it.

Fordham isn't a perv, not a guy who'd grope a girl who goes for help after school. Why did Nat see him when she was meant to be seeing me? Rang, but the machine was on. Thought of e-mailing, but she never answers properly.

Forgot all about the Disney girl until I started writing this. I looked up Harris in the phone book. There are hundreds of them, but none in Burngreave.

Her name's Cate, not Kate, short for Caitlin. Harris is her mum's surname, which is why I couldn't find her in the book. Found this out when she wrote down her mobile number for me on the bus this a.m. Saw her again after school in the library, head stuck in a book. Her dad didn't show so she caught up with me on the bus. We walked home from town. She's not like the girls round here, but nervy, mysterious (spoilt daddy's girl, she says) and sharp – brighter than Nat who says brains scare people off. As I was trying to kiss her goodbye, Cat turned her head slightly, I only caught the cheek. Don't know if she meant to or not.

When I got in Mum told me Nat phoned, wants me to go round tomorrow. Mum asked what was happening. Didn't tell her, not really. Rumours at school today but I avoided them. When people asked where Nat was, I said she was ill. 'Yeah, I'd be off ill if somebody had caught me having sex with a teacher in the Year Nine common room,' Tom Berber said.

Natasha has to talk to the police, doesn't want to. Pat said 'Persuade her. You can't let a man like that get away with it.' Then she told me what Nat says happened: how Fordham asked to see her, went on about how beautiful she was, how he couldn't keep his hands off her. Before she knew it, he had a hand on her arse and, when she tried to move away, grabbed her, tried to kiss her, stuck his free hand up her shirt. Pat said all this real matter of fact, expecting me to be angry. And I was, but only sort *of. It sounded like he had three hands, for a start. Did he rip her shirt on the way in, or the way out? And why didn't she tell me about it straight away?*

'How does she say it finished?' I asked.

'Somebody interrupted them.'

'Who?'

'She doesn't know. Fordham heard the door open and let go. Natasha rushed out of the other door. Then she went and found you.'

So there's a witness, one who can say what really happened. Another teacher, probably, one who'll protect Fordham.

Spent ages with Nat. She doesn't want to talk to the police. But if she pulls out, she might be expelled for making false allegations. So I went over her story with her again and again until it made sense. Least it's no longer her word against his. Witness must have seen something. Forgot all about ringing Cate.

Cate's the weirdest, brightest, sexiest girl I've ever met. After spending yesterday with Natasha, all me-me-me and trust-me games (more I think about it, more I reckon she must have given F a come-on – no teacher would take such a risk otherwise) seeing Cate was like breathing clean air. We walked round the graveyard behind her house. She said she loved graveyards and read loads of the inscriptions to me. Whenever I thought it was getting serious, she'd make some kind of joke. Realised she was flirting with me.

I don't know how to flirt. I can recognise the red signals Nat gives out when I get the wrong idea, but I think I'd need a 'Yes' written in ten-foot-high neon letters. Eventually worked up the nerve to ask Cate if she had a boyfriend in the village where she used to live. 'Not a serious one', she said, then asked how many girlfriends I'd had. Rather than give the roundest number of all, I said 'nobody serious' and she gave me this melting, vulnerable look which meant I was allowed to kiss her. So I did. Then she made me look at some more gravestones before we kissed again. And again. And again.

This is special. Mustn't let on, got to play cool. Nat always tell me I can come to her for advice on stuff like this, but now's not the time. She'd probably tell me to slow down, act hard to get. I can't play those games.

What's great with Cate is we can be really silly together. She got me playing this dressing-up game. Mum walked in on me showing off in some old underpants, jumped to conclusion we were having sex. When Cat ran off I told her we'd never done anything but kiss (nearly true) and I was serious about Cate so she had to be nice to her. Mum said she'd do her best, then said Pat rang earlier and the police want to talk to me. I don't want to talk to them.

Cate came round when Mum was out. This time, both of us were next to naked – I was too nervous to suggest doing it. Dork. After a while she started asking about Nat. Felt weird. Didn't want to give Cate any reason to be jealous of Nat. Admitted I'd probably see her at the weekend when Cate has to go stay with her mum. Agreed to e-mail. When Mum got in, Mel told her I'd had Cate round again and she gave me the big lecture about condoms.

The police interview took about twenty minutes. This horrible little puke-green room in the station down the road on Sunday afternoon. Since I'm over sixteen, they were allowed to iv me alone. Sergeant wanted to know what state Nat was in, to check her story against mine. Since I'd spent half Saturday with her, that wasn't difficult. Then the DS – bad haircut, bad breath, about twenty-five – got all matey with me, trying to be man-to-man.

'She's a tasty thing, isn't she?'

'I don't . . .'

'If I put myself in this Fordham's position. She's practically legal. If you met her down the pub or at a *party, you wouldn't think twice about trying it on.'*

'He's her teacher. He knows how old she is.'

'And that's what riled you, wasn't it?'

'I don't understand.'

'The way her mother tells it, you were Natasha's first boyfriend – just thirteen years old. Probably lost your sweet little cherries together, did you? But she moved on to older guys, ones who didn't treat her as well as you did. You were there to pick up the pieces, like when she had that abortion a year ago. And you like doing that, don't you? So when she told you that this Fordham had got a little flirty with her, you persuaded her to talk it up, turn it into a much more serious allegation. Because you were jealous. It's understandable.'

Shook my head, trying to control my temper. 'That's so much bullshit.'

The DS got more crude. 'Look, son, I'd feel exactly the same way in your position. You wish you were still shagging her and hate anyone else who might be. But this is serious stuff. A man could lose his career, go to prison. Meanwhile, you turned sixteen at the start of the month. Natasha might get away with playing the spoilt kid – she's still got six months to go. You, on the other hand, could be looking at a charge of criminal conspiracy.'

'You've got it all wrong,' I told him. 'Natasha and I never

went out, not that way. I'm her friend, that's all. I've got a girlfriend. And Nat, she didn't want to talk about it at first. I got her to because I could see she was upset. Yes, I told her to report Fordham. So did her mum. But Nat wouldn't do it unless it was true – I mean, why else would anyone put themselves through something like this?'

The DS played the silent thing on me, waiting to see if I'd add anything. Then he said: 'I'll offer you an alternative view of that afternoon. Your friend Natasha has spent the summer building up this fantasy about Fordham. He was very nice to her last year, admits as much. Her teachers knew about the abortion and were watching out for her, especially given the stick some of the other kids were giving her. But Natasha takes this the wrong way, decides he wants to be more than a teacher to her. So, first chance she gets, your Natasha catches him on her own, pops a couple of buttons on her blouse – 'oh what an accident, they've broken. Tell me, do you like what you see, Sir?' And Fordham, who's got a daughter her age by the way, he tells her no way and walks out. So you see her, and she's upset. You get a story out of her. Only she gives it you arse-over-face. And next thing you know, she's convinced herself that he popped those buttons and she turned him down. How does that sound?'

Crude, but scarily convincing. I'd thought as much myself,

only, in my version, Fordham was tempted, maybe copped a feel before going into the moral no, I'm a teacher, bit. He's a dad, with a teenager. Does that make a difference?

'Well, son? I know you might find it hard to think that anybody could resist your childhood sweetheart, but the man has a lot to lose. Can you think of anything which is going to convince me that she didn't make most of it up?'

'You don't know Fordham,' I said. 'He taught me all last year and I saw the way he looked at Nat. And there were little things, like he'd stand too close to her, linger near her as people were leaving a lesson so they'd be alone in the classroom. If you think she's lying, ask yourself this. What teacher in his right mind arranges to see a girl who looks like Nat, with her history, on her own, after school, like that? He thought he was in there. When it turned out he wasn't, he still reckoned he'd get away with it because he saw Nat as the school slag. He didn't think she'd have the nerve to report him. Only she did, and if you don't take her word for it and put him in court over what happened, then you deserve to lose your job!'

That shut him up. On the way out, he shook my hand.

'Nothing personal, you understand. We have to play devil's advocate in these situations.' Then he gave me a look that seemed to say: If I have my way, we'll do the bastard.

OCTOBER

C and I finally had the house to ourselves and made good use of it. Just when we're starkers, she gets clingy and jealous and finally starts crying, insisting she's worried about how close I am to Nat. So, to prove it isn't so, I showed her some of this diary, (nothing about her. Checked before she looked). Everything she read, I'd already told the police. Yet I felt naked. I was letting her see right into my mind, but she won't let me deep into hers, not even in the long e-mail she sent from Parwich last w/e.

Cate was away for the weekend so Nat came over. Funny, now I'm with Cate, it's easier to be around Nat. I can have her in my room without wanting to jump her. She seems more relaxed with me, too. She's seeing someone and says school isn't too bad now.

'People talk behind my back, give me funny looks. But they've always done that. Except for you. In a funny way, it's easier to get on with work. Wish we had a better English teacher though.'

'Yeah. Fordham's a pretty good teacher.'

'Was,' Natasha said. 'They won't let him teach again.'

'Even if it doesn't go to trial?'

'Oh but it is,' Nat told me. 'That's why I came round. The police rang this morning. They charged Dan yesterday.'

Talked a bit about Cate. Seemed strange discussing her with another girl. Still Cate talks about Nat to me, guess it's OK. Nat'd like to get to know her.

'That'd be good. She doesn't have any other real friends in school.'

'None at all?'

'There's this girl called Holly, but I don't think Cate sees her outside school. Cate slags her off sometimes.'

'Doesn't mean they're not friends. I was always slagging you off to my friends back in Year Nine. They used to call you my lapdog. But I never meant it. I just wanted to look cool, to go out with older boys. And I'm not friendly with any of those girls now. You're the only person at school I talk to. Maybe Cate and me would get on. I mean, we've got liking you in common.'

I wasn't sure if Cate would want to be Nat's friend and said so. Told her I reckoned female friendships are much more confusing than males ones.

'You can say that again,' Nat told me. 'But there's one thing that's even more confusing.'

'What's that?'

'Boy/girl friendships.'

In Broomhill today, about to go into Record Collector saw Mr Fordham and Ms Grant, standing really close together.

Thought they'd split up when she moved to London. If Fordham's still with her, why would he make a pass at Nat?

Cate wrote, saying she loves me. I've told her the same. It's true. It's fucking great. Can't stop caring about Nat, too. Not sexually – I hate that she must have been with lots of blokes (never dared ask how many) – that's a real turn-off. What I'd really like is to sleep with Cate when she's ready and for that to be it, for ever and ever, neither of us ever having done it or wanting to do it with anybody else.

I suppose that makes me a hopeless romantic.

C's dad late back from London so I went over and we did it. I shouldn't have been upset she wasn't a virgin but I was (think I hid it well enough). She kept giving me all these hints about the wild things she'd done in her last year of her old school – thought she was talking about drugs and stealing. I was mad for it, then finished almost as soon as I started. Cate seemed uncomfy with the whole thing. She let me screw her and I don't know if I still love her. How weird is that?

Nat asked whether I'd come round after school, stay for tea. There was something she wanted to tell me. I told her Cate was meant to be coming round at eight.

'I'll get my dad to drive you home in time,' she promised.

When I got there, she wanted to know about the police interview.

'That was ages ago.'

'I had a second interview. Did they interview you again too?'

'No. I told them everything I knew the first time.'

'Including how many people I've slept with?'

'No! I don't know anything about that. And even if I did . . .'

Nat started reciting names in this low monotone, presumably the names the police had given her: 'James Coulter, Mark Long, Darren Thomas, Salif Hitu'. It went on and on. The list was absurd – half the lads on it were in our year and Nat never went out with anybody from our year unless you count me, which I don't.

'Do you know how many people on that list I've slept with?' Nat asked me.

I really didn't want to hear the answer.

'Not one. I only went out with a couple of them. The police say that, if they didn't have this witness, they'd drop the case. And I don't know how much he saw. He was only in the room a moment. Mr Fordham didn't notice him.'

'Who was it? Did they tell you?'

Nat ignored the question. 'They're making me out to

be this . . . this whore. And it's so far from . . . if I told people at school how few people I've done it with, they wouldn't credit it. I told your friend Cate, trying to get her on my side. I don't think she believed me.'

She stopped talking. My jaw must have dropped wide open.

'It's all right. I didn't tell her that the first bloke I did it with was you.'

27

People lie all the time. I lie. You lie. Natasha lies. Dan lies. I thought Aaron always told the truth. I couldn't remember him saying out loud that he'd not had sex with Natasha – but he'd told me he'd never been out with her, that she always preferred older blokes and wasn't interested in him. He'd let me think he hadn't slept with her (or anyone). But he had, back when Natasha was younger than I was.

Natasha had told me that she'd only slept with two blokes, and she'd been in love with both of them. Which meant she'd been in love with Aaron. Which meant, somewhere inside, she still was. And probably would be again.

The weekend kept going from bad to worse. Mum left me with Daisy while she slept, then went shopping with Trevor. In the evening, he cooked. Mum, who'd hardly spoken all day, went to bed at nine, saying something about having to get up early with Daisy.

'I guess I'll go to my room,' I told Trevor.

'You're going to leave me to watch TV on my own?'

'You know I hate football.'

'It's not on for an hour. Stay and talk to me.'

I had nothing better to do. I didn't want to phone Aaron as he might be round at Natasha's. I decided to try something on.

'Do you mind if I have a smoke first?'

'As long as it's a straight. You might as well smoke in here. It's cold outside.'

He had a coal fire going and I used it as an ashtray. I wondered about the way he'd used the word 'straight'. How old was Trevor? He was born in the sixties, so too young to have been any kind of hippy. While I smoked, he lectured me.

'Caitlin, I know at your age people are pretty self-obsessed, but you must have noticed your mum's not very happy.'

This is it I thought. He's having an affair. He's going to leave her, like he left his first wife. But it wasn't that.

'I managed to persuade her to go to a doctor. He's diagnosed her as suffering from post-natal depression.'

'But Daisy's nearly eighteen months old!'

'Depression can last for years, especially when it's undiagnosed. The doctor's prescribed her some anti-depressants but it'll take a while for her to get on an even keel.'

I struggled to take this in: both of my parents on Prozac.

'I think I owe you an apology,' Trevor said.

'What for?'

'Last year, when you were acting up all the time – the way you dressed, the piercings, the bullying, the drugs, the car, your whole attitude . . . your mother got so upset. At times she was almost suicidal, impossible to live with. And I blamed you.'

'It was my fault. I did those things.'

'I know. But your mother wasn't really there for you. And neither was I. I hated you for coming between us and our beautiful new baby. That was terrible of me.'

I didn't know what to say. I was used to kids at school saying they hated me, not adults.

'Since you've been gone, a lot of things have shifted into perspective. And look at you – you're so beautiful, your mother's daughter. And I could tell when I met him that Aaron's a really nice guy. School seems to be going fine. But any time you want to come back – any time, for a weekend, a week, a month, forever, you'll always be welcome here. That comes from me, not just your mother.'

Then he put his arms round me and kissed me on the forehead. I hugged him back, but only for a moment, because he seemed to expect it.

28

On Monday I was hanging around in the library waiting for Aaron when Natasha came in. She was trying to give up smoking, so we hadn't talked for a while. It was the first time I'd seen her in the library since the day it happened and she looked ill at ease, out of place. Then she spotted me and came over.

'Aaron's had to go to the dentist, poor lamb. He asked me to tell you because your mobile's switched off.'

'Thanks for letting me know.'

'No sweat.' Natasha put a hand on my shoulder. 'Why don't I walk with you?'

'Sure,' I said, still acting friendly to see what I could find out. It would only be a short walk. We caught different buses.

'Aaron says you like messing with people's heads,' Natasha told me as we got to the bottom of the stairs by the library.

'Sometimes.' I hesitated. 'Depends who the people are.'

'Don't look to your right, but creepy Michael's standing there. He likes to watch. Know what I mean? Play along.'

Natasha put her left arm around my shoulder, pushing me gently against the wall. Then she pressed up close and kissed me full on the lips, opening her mouth a little. For a moment, I thought she was going to stick her tongue in. Then I remembered that I was meant to be playing along, so I opened my mouth and tried to reach around her waist, and I ended up feeling her bottom. Natasha wriggled a little before she pulled away and smiled.

'Don't look back,' she whispered, giving me a loving look. 'And whatever you do, don't laugh, not yet.'

Once we were out of the school building, Natasha began to giggle. Next thing, we were both laughing like maniacs. Other kids turned to look at us but Natasha didn't seem to care.

'You should have seen his face! Sweet.'

Natasha only calmed down as we neared her bus stop, where there was a big queue.

'You're a good kisser,' she told me. 'I've had a lot worse.'

'I get plenty of practice,' I told her.

She joined the queue. Still flushed, I walked along the path towards my bus stop. I wondered whose head Natasha really meant to mess with: mine, or Michael's. Was he even there? I hadn't noticed him before Natasha did what she did. It was only when I was lying in bed that night, unable to sleep, that I worked the whole thing out. *Michael likes to watch.*

29

I bumped into Holly in the library after school. We didn't talk much at tutor time any more, each keeping ourselves to ourselves. So I was surprised when she sat down next to me.

'Your dad picking you up?'

'That's right,' I lied. 'Taking me to Meadowhall. You?'

'Overdue history coursework,' Holly said, but didn't get any work out. 'Are you still going out with Aaron?'

'Far as I know,' I said, coolly. 'Why?'

'Thought you ought to know that there's talk . . . probably only shit stirring, but . . .'

She hesitated, trying to choose the right words, so I cut to the chase. 'Me snogging Natasha Clark?'

'It's true then?'

I was about to have a go at Holly. Then I saw that she looked concerned, not like she was after gossip.

'We were winding somebody up, that's all.'

'You chose an odd person to wind somebody up with.'

'Natasha's not so bad.' I didn't know why I was defending her.

'You believe the story about Fordham molesting her?'

'I don't know.' As I said it, I realised I was telling the truth. I still hated Natasha for that, but I didn't know what I thought about anything any more. That was why I'd stayed behind after school.

'You ask me, she offered it him on a plate, but he turned her down. So she's getting her own back. *Hell hath no fury like a woman spurned*. Shakespeare.'

Holly, having given me something to think about, sat on her own. I tried to read for a few minutes. There were no teachers around. They'd either gone home or were in meetings. I went to one of the reference shelves and looked up Holly's Shakespeare line in a book of quotations. It wasn't there. She must have got it wrong.

Trying to act casual, I left the library and looked for Michael. I had a cover story – a missing pen I'd left in the Year Nine common room at afternoon break. He wouldn't know I didn't have any lessons in that room.

I found him in the last place I looked, the staff room. The door was propped open with a bin and Michael was sitting in one of the easy chairs, having a brew. When I put my head round the door, he started. Then he saw who I was and relaxed. I put on my best, pleading voice.

'. . . I'm almost certain I left it there. Would you open the room up, please?'

Michael was in his late twenties, with a slight limp and a swollen, wobbly jaw – I don't know what caused either of them. He was married – or, at least, wore a ring – and had a thick Barnsley accent. As I'd hoped, he didn't take much persuading. He even stayed and helped me look (the pen was just under a curtain, where no-one in the last class was likely to have spotted and stolen it).

I spoke without looking at him. 'This is where it happened, isn't it? Natasha told me everything.'

'Did she now?'

'She said you saw everything. You're an important witness.'

'I see a lot of things,' he replied, slowly. 'Hear them too. People often forget I'm about. They leave the door open and they see right through me, if you know what I mean.'

'I do. I feel like that sometimes.'

'I doubt it. Pretty girl like you.'

This was getting a little creepy. The way he was looking at me, I was sure Michael had seen Natasha snogging me the day before. He bent down to look for my pen. Michael was near the curtain already, getting too warm, too quickly.

'What did you see?' I asked.

'More than either of them would have liked.'

'Was Natasha telling the truth? Did you see Mr Fordham force himself on her?'

'I didn't see that, no.'

'What did you see?'

Michael didn't reply. Why should he tell me? I was coming on way too strong. Michael considered for a moment, his hand moving beneath the curtain where the pen was concealed. Then he pulled his hand back and used it to lean on. With his free hand, he pointed out of the window.

'I was standing over there. I saw the girl, your friend, standing close to the teacher. He had an arm around her. She looked upset, only I couldn't tell what with, or even be sure who he was. The police wanted me to say he pulled her up towards him, but she could just as easily have been reaching up to kiss him. I thought best to ignore it. Best to ignore most things like that. But windows were open and I heard her shout, 'Drop dead. I never want to see you again.' Then your dad said something I couldn't hear and she came charging out, so fast I didn't think she'd noticed me. Only you tell me she did.'

'I think she found out about you from the police.'

'I see.' Michael swept the curtain aside, revealing my pen. Is this it?'

'Yes.' I took the pen and thanked him. Only then did I realise what he'd just said. 'How did you know that Mr Fordham's my father?'

Michael stood up, unfolding his awkward frame. 'Told you: I overhear things. Like Miss Jackson telling Mrs Taylor what effect this was having on Fordham's daughter. She were saying how you hid things really well . . . so well, it's scary, she said. When I heard that, I remembered how you came looking for Fordham, night he got suspended. Now you make up this excuse to talk to me today. Doesn't take Sherlock Holmes to guess who you are.'

'Do you think my father . . . did what she says?'

'You're asking the wrong person.' Michael walked me to the door and locked it behind us. 'But the way he was with that girl . . .' He thought better of finishing the sentence. I didn't care what he thought. I knew what had happened. Michael had seen what Natasha wanted him to see.

30

Dan had been to the doctor's.

'He reduced the meds, said I seemed to be coping pretty well, considering. I told him about the drinking binges. He said I was unlikely to have done my liver any permanent damage.'

'I want to ask you something.'

'Oh yes. What?' My father's face was blank, innocent, not his usual self. The last two months had stripped him of much of the confidence he'd built up since becoming a teacher.

'What grudge does Natasha have against you that could persuade her to make up such an allegation?'

Dan seemed surprised I was asking him this again, now, after all these weeks of our not discussing it.

'Does she have to have a grudge?' he asked.

'Yes. Otherwise her lying doesn't make sense.'

'My solicitor says the same thing. But not all behaviour does make sense. Especially – you'll have to forgive this – the behaviour of girls in the middle of adolescence.'

'I suppose not. But I think Natasha knew what she was doing. I spoke to Michael.'

'Who's Michael?'

'The assistant caretaker, the one who saw you kissing Natasha.'

'He's the witness? How the hell did you find that out?'

'I asked around. He didn't see you grope her. He didn't see you push her away either. You didn't push her away, did you?'

I watched Dan as his eyes shifted into sharper focus. 'I don't . . . I don't . . . no, that's a lie. I do remember. I'm only human, Cate. She reached up, pressed against me, kissed me. It was . . . nice.'

I hate the word 'nice': it's so bland, so *nice*. What Dan had said hung in the air between us. He gave me a nervous look, worried he was stirring up too much trouble. He was waiting for a judgement, an eruption of my famous teenage temper. He'd never really seen it, only heard about it. But I wasn't angry. What he'd told me made sense. He'd been tempted. More than tempted.

'It didn't go any further, I swear.'

'Michael said you had an arm around her.'

Dan didn't reply.

'And then she started shouting at you. What spurred that?'

'Natasha . . . tried to put her tongue in my mouth. I saw sense, pulled back.'

I tried to stay calm, cool, to be lawyerly. 'But you didn't grope her, break her buttons?'

'No. She must have done that herself, after she'd left.'

'Why? Why swear at you like that? because you wouldn't let her put her tongue down your throat?'

'I wish I knew. You can't imagine how many times I've gone over it in my mind.'

I thought I knew. 'Can't you see? You might not have known that Michael was outside, but Natasha did. When you turned her down, she made sure he heard what she wanted him to hear. Natasha set you up.'

31

'Often,' Aaron said. 'I feel like you're older than me.'

'The word's *mature*, not *older*. Girls go out with boys two years older because there's a two year maturity gap. So, next week, when we're only a year apart, I'll be the more mature one.'

'I'm floored by your logic,' Aaron said, putting his hand up my school skirt.

There was still an hour before his mother came home. Downstairs, I could hear his sister listening to the radio. I wondered whether it would be different to have a full sister rather than a half sister. If they'd had another child, maybe my mum and dad would have stayed together.

When I got home, it struck me: neither of us had mentioned Natasha once. Foolishly, I thought that was a good thing.

Dan had a visitor. Ed Lloyd, a History teacher from school. Like John the ex-teacher told me, when a teacher was suspended, the head had to designate a member of staff to keep the teacher in touch with what was happening at work (never mind that I went to the school). Dan wasn't meant to talk to any of the teachers other than Ed, which was unfair: most of his friends worked there. And this was only Ed's second visit.

'How do you think he's doing?' Mr Lloyd asked, when Dan was in the loo. 'Everybody's worried about him.'

'Except the ones who think he did it.'

'Nobody believes Natasha Clark. They can't understand why she holds such a grudge against him, that's all. Can you?'

'Maybe she just flipped,' I said, although the more I got to know Natasha, the less she seemed like somebody who would freak that way. She was too cool, too calculating.

'I suppose. Your father says there are allegations like this all the time, hundreds a year. Malicious pranks mainly.'

'Right,' I sneered. 'So he should feel better because it happens all the time?'

'And only four percent of those cases end in conviction.'

You can prove anything with statistics, Dan always says. I've read most crimes don't even get reported, never mind punished. In which case, maybe most teachers got away with it.

'The way I see it,' Mr Lloyd went on. 'Natasha Clark built up a fixation on your father, one that came to a head during the summer holidays. The autumn term started. At the first opportunity, she threw herself at him. When he didn't respond, Natasha "flipped" as you say – convinced herself it all happened the other way round. She rejected him.'

When Dan came back, my mind drifted off. I was still trying to get my head around the possibility of Aaron being responsible for Natasha's pregnancy. Trouble was, I couldn't ask him about it. He'd know I'd read his diary.

'I'm sure it won't come to trial,' Mr Lloyd was telling Dan.

'Say it doesn't,' Dan says. 'Say they drop the charges. The school can still sack me, or force me to resign. According to the people at the union, it's up to the governors: if they decide that "on the balance of possibilities" I behaved unprofessionally, they can sack me without compensation.'

'And if they don't?'

'Then they force Natasha to move schools and that's the end of it.'

32

My birthday was on a Saturday. Janet and Melanie were away, visiting a friend in Exeter. Aaron had the house to himself for the night. So it was official: fifteen was the new sixteen. We could sleep together with Janet's blessing.

Another first: we had time to do it more than once. Before the M and S meal Aaron's mum left in for us. Then again after. Dan hadn't put me on a curfew. I could go home whenever I wanted. But all I wanted was to stay in Aaron's arms. It was the most relaxing, refreshing feeling – much better than sex – sinking into the soft, cool flesh of a boy who loved you.

He dozed a little. I didn't. When he woke, he drank lager and I sipped diet coke. And we talked, taking it in turns to tell each other everything. Not just how we felt about each other, but everything. That night, I couldn't lie to him. I was working up to telling him the truth about Dan being my dad. He'd understand. But then Aaron spoiled it.

'Tell me about the guy you were with before,' he said. 'I won't be jealous, I promise.'

'You really don't want to hear about it,' I said, playing with the silver ring he'd given me.

'There was more than one before me?'

'No, only one. And he ...' I didn't mean to, but I started to cry. 'He took advantage. I didn't know better.'

'He sounds like a creep,' Aaron said, holding me as I wiped my face. 'I didn't mean to upset you. Your turn. Ask me anything.'

I took him at his word and went in deep. 'You let me think you were a virgin, but I don't think you were.'

'Why? Because I'm so good at it?'

'It was something Natasha told me.'

I let that hang there, wishing the light was on so that I could see his eyes.

'She told you?'

'No, but you just did.'

He didn't say anything else for a long time. I let the silence linger until it became uncomfortable. He broke first.

'We were always mates but that was all. Her mum used to say she wished Nat was going out with me rather than the scum she did date. It happened when this lad in Year Eleven dumped Nat because she wouldn't let him screw her. Nat was really broken up about it. I think she slept with me out of revenge – Nat's big on revenge – to prove some kind of point. We only did it that once. I asked her to go out with me but she wanted to stay just friends. Then we found out she was pregnant.'

'Who else knows?' I asked.

'That it was mine? Nobody guessed. Even her mum and dad thought it was the Year Eleven lad. I'm not the sort of guy you expect someone like Natasha to sleep with.'

'Don't run yourself down. I sleep with you.'

'Yeah, but you're an outsider like me. Whereas Natasha, she's part of the gang, always has friends to go on the pull with. Or she did have. Until one of them spilt the beans about her being pregnant at the beginning of the summer holidays.'

'Ouch. On purpose?'

Aaron thought for a moment before continuing, in a different, more remote voice. 'It was in an English lesson. Fordham wanted someone to read the section of *Tess of the D'Urbervilles* just after Tess finds out she's pregnant. Emma Cave calls out to *get Natasha to do it. She knows what it's like.* And Fordham gets Emma to repeat what she just said. Nat rushes out of the room. Soon it's all over the school. Mrs Taylor asks to see Natasha, to offer her counselling. Can you imagine how crap she felt?'

'So that's it,' I blurted out.

'What?'

'Why Natasha hates Mr Fordham. You said it: Natasha's big on revenge. It was Mr Fordham's fault that everyone found out about her getting pregnant.'

Aaron was indignant. 'Natasha hates Fordham because he felt her up and told her he wanted to give her one. Why are you so interested in Fordham anyhow?' He paused. 'Oh, I forgot, he lives on your street.'

'How do you know that?' I asked, trying to stop my voice going all whiney.

'That camper van. It's definitely his. He's got a Grateful Dead sticker on the back window.'

He was right. My father had seen the Grateful Dead play before I was born. He'd never stopped going on about it since.

'Do you see him around?' Aaron wanted to know.

'Fordham? I see a guy getting into the VW van now and then. I wouldn't know if it's him.'

'He has a girlfriend – young and skinny, short blonde hair, really pretty face.'

'Not any more.' I shouldn't have let those words slip out either.

'Pardon?'

'I mean, I haven't seen her around for a while.'

'But you know who I mean.'

'I think so.'

'She used to work at our school.'

As the conversation went on, we'd stopped whispering like lovers and begun talking in a normal tone of voice. Abruptly, Aaron put the light on. I took this as a cue to get dressed. I needed to go before I accidentally gave anything else away.

'I'll have to tell Natasha,' he said.

'Tell her what?'

'That you know. We both promised never to tell anyone. But it'll be cool. She likes you. She's happy I'm with you.'

Natasha, Natasha, Natasha, Natasha: we'd made love twice and still the thing he cared about most was Natasha.

33

'Here you are,' Natasha said. 'Late birthday present.'

'Cool.' The gift was a black plastic lighter, with a white skull and crossbones and the word 'Death' written on it (*Death* – as in the brand of cigarettes). It seemed odd that Natasha was the only person in school who knew I'd just had a birthday.

We lit each other up. Other girls (the smokers were mainly girls) clustered further down the boundary hedge, occasionally throwing glances at the notorious Natasha Clark. Natasha had lost weight and wore no make-up. Her cheekbones were visible. Her eyes had a hollow, haunted quality. I asked how long it was since she'd started smoking again but Natasha didn't reply.

'He told me,' she said instead.

'I won't tell anybody.'

'He says I gave you a hint.'

'Not really. I guessed.'

'You bluffed him. I'll bet you're good at lying.'

'Not as good as you.' These words slipped out, but Natasha took no offence.

'Boys don't expect girls to lie, but we have to, all the time.'

'I don't know about all the time,' I said, though I did.

'Sometimes you lie so as not to hurt somebody. And sometimes a lie is better at getting justice than the truth.'

'You're talking about Mr Fordham,' I said.

Natasha grinned. 'If I had an ounce of conscience,' she boasted, but in a self-mocking way, 'I'd feel guilty.'

She started to say more, then stopped herself. But I'd found out all I needed to know. My dad was innocent. All this time, a part of me had half-believed he'd done it or, at least, done something. Now I was relieved, but I also felt numb.

'You don't know anything about Mr Fordham,' Natasha went on, stubbing her cigarette out. Then she added, 'I didn't hint to you, not once. I wanted Aaron to be happy and I wanted you to know I wasn't going to keep him on a string any more. Hinting about what happened wasn't necessary.'

'Did it really happen?' I asked. 'Or did you sleep

with Aaron because you were already pregnant and needed him to be around for you?'

Natasha simulated shock. 'You really are devious,' she said. 'What do you want? The bloody sheet? Aaron can't believe you worked it out. Neither can I. I reckon you read his diary.'

Now she was calling my bluff. Natasha looked me straight in the eyes.

'I thought so,' she said. 'That was a big mistake.'

34

I wanted to run home to Dan, to tell him what I'd found out, that I knew why Natasha had lied. But first I texted Aaron and arranged to meet him. I needed to explain about his diary before Natasha told him. Aaron would understand – after all, he'd already shown me some of the diary. Even if he didn't, I'd apologise so much, and cry so hard, he was bound to forgive me. I only did it because I wasn't sure whether he really loved me.

Dan was dozing on the sofa when I got in. I woke him.

'I spoke to Natasha Clark today.'

'You spoke to her? You shouldn't be going near—'

'I've spoken to her lots of times,' I told him. 'I've been trying to help you. Today I found out something.'

'What?'

'Aaron told me about this lesson a year ago . . .'

Dan struggled to take it all in so I had to go over everything twice.

'I barely recall . . . I think I was distracted, which is why I asked her to repeat what she'd said. Later, I heard the story that Natasha had had an abortion, but the school was never officially told, so I'm not sure where it surfaced first.' He thought for a moment. 'Yes, now you come to mention it, Natasha did walk out. But I don't know what this has to do with . . .'

'Don't you see? It explains why she made it all up.'

'Does it?'

'All the time I thought you were leaving something out. It didn't make enough sense that she suddenly turned on you because she was a woman spurned . . .'

'The saying isn't a woman *spurned*,' Dan said. 'I've had reason to reread those lines. It's *scorned*. They're from Congreve:

"Heaven has no rage like love to hatred turned,

Nor hell a fury, like a woman scorned." '

He stopped, as though he was just starting to take in what I'd told him.

'You thought I was leaving something out? I can hardly blame you. But I'm not sure this makes as much difference as you think. I've had some good news though—'

'I haven't finished,' I interrupted. 'I wasn't sure I believed you until this afternoon, when Natasha more or less admitted that she'd made the whole thing up. Now I know you didn't do it.'

After I'd said this, Dan hugged me, even though we never did hugs. Then he told me the good news he'd had earlier. He'd spoken to his solicitor that afternoon.

'Seems the Crown Prosecution Service are almost certain to drop the case. There's not enough hard evidence. The real issue is what the school governors decide. All they have to go on is the balance of probabilities. If I can convince them of what you've just told me, I'll be back at school by Christmas.'

'I hope so,' I told him.

'This deserves a drink.' Dan went to the kitchen and got one. 'To my beautiful, brilliant daughter,' he said, raising a large vodka and tonic.

I took a small bow. My mobile rang.

'I need to see you now,' Aaron said. 'Can I come round?'

'It's not a good time,' I said, looking at my smiling father. I wasn't going to get those two together until Dan had been reinstated. I looked outside. It was a mild, November day.

'We could meet in the place in the corner,' I told Aaron.

I meant the corner of the graveyard.

'OK,' Aaron said. 'Fifteen minutes.'

35

Dan made me stay until he'd phoned his union official. Barry said my explanation for Natasha's behaviour would probably hold water with the school governors. He even spoke to me for several minutes.

'And what did Natasha do to the girl who broke her trust?'

'I don't know. But I'm meeting my boyfriend now. I'll ask,' I said.

Aaron was waiting when I got there. I reached up to kiss him but he took a step backwards.

'You read my diary,' he said.

'You've spoken to Natasha already,' I mumbled. She must have phoned him as soon as she got home.

'Why?' he asked.

'To see if I could trust you,' I said. 'To see if I could trust Natasha with you.'

'I thought we loved each other. Without trust, there's no love.'

'I do love you,' I said. 'But I was worried that you were still in love with Natasha.'

'So you read my diary and discovered I really was in love with you.'

'Yes,' I said. There was no point in explaining what I'd read between the lines. 'I'm sorry.'

'I'm sorry, too,' Aaron said. 'I thought you were really straight with me. Now I'm not sure if I ever knew you.'

'Aaron, please.' His face remained hard, untouched. I began to plead. 'I love you. I did a stupid thing, but there's no damage done.'

'No damage! I promised Nat that what happened would always be our secret.'

'She lies to you. All that stuff about Fordham, for instance. She made it up, to get back at him for letting everybody find out about the abortion. She more or less admitted it to me.'

'I'm not interested in Fordham. You don't know anything about me and Nat, and you never will.'

'I'm sorry, I—'

'I don't want to hear it, Cate. I'm finishing with you.'

I was back in the house five minutes later, chucked. Dan was refreshing his drink. I asked if I could have one, too.

36

Around Christmas, I began to have problems sleeping. Even when I was at my worst, the year before, I never had trouble in that department. If anything, I used to sleep more when I was depressed. Much more. Yet now I couldn't get to sleep.

I tried everything. I thought booze was meant to be an anti-depressant but it set my heart racing. So did weed, when I could get it. What worked best was reading until the words stopped going in. Then I'd put the light out and try to drift off. But thoughts would creep up on me. I'd try to go blank. It would kind of work. Then another random thought would flick across my mind and I'd think, *oh shit I'm having a thought* and I'd be wide awake again.

Sometimes I got a bit nearer. Random images would play at the back of my brain – strange, cartoon images, or TV characters, even people I knew. And I'd think, *oh great, I'm starting to have a dream*, then wake up.

Eventually, somehow, in the darkest, quietest hours, I'd get off, only to be woken around dawn by the smallest noise, the need to pee, or Dan snoring in the next room. And that'd be it – wide awake with only three or at most four hours' sleep and no chance of getting back off. I developed these dark lines under my eyes, as though nature had always intended for me to be a Goth. It didn't matter. I'd stopped caring what I looked like.

I wasn't staying awake because I was obsessing about Aaron. I still loved him and everything, but I'd known all along: he was Natasha's. There was no point in trying to get him back. It was a waste of time beating myself up over how I shouldn't have read his diary. *My bad*. Get over it.

The school managed Dan's reinstatement gracefully. Natasha was found a place at a nearby school where she could do the same exam courses. Everybody there thought she'd just moved into the area. The Crown Prosecution Service dropped the charges against Dan and the governors immediately agreed that he had no case to answer. So there was no trial, no opportunity for Dan to tell Natasha what a mess she'd made of his life. He rang Jo to give her the good news but she'd moved without telling him, which was a message in itself: she'd finished with him for good this time.

I tried e-mailing Aaron to explain myself. He didn't reply. When I called up, Janet wouldn't put me through, but explained: 'You invaded his privacy, Cate. He feels he can't trust you.'

One time I even tried going round there. His sister answered the door. 'He's at Natasha's,' she told me. 'As far as you're concerned, if you call, he'll always be at Natasha's.'

At school, I never saw him. I guess I was easy to avoid.

In assembly, the head announced that my dad would be returning next term.

'Mr Fordham has had to deal with a difficult situation, which he did with great dignity. He returns without any doubt cast on his character. I expect everybody to treat him with tact and respect. Those of you who know something of the situation may have noticed that the person whose allegations brought about Mr Fordham's absence no longer attends this school. I trust that this speaks for itself.'

The school didn't issue any statement to the press, not wanting to rake over the embers, remind people of the scandal. But the press found out anyway. They published a paragraph about Dan's reinstatement, saying that he had been cleared of any wrongdoing. He slid quietly back into school during the last week of term. It was, he said, like he'd never been away.

37

Two months later, just before spring half term, I was at The Crucible theatre, where Dan had taken me to see a play, *Two Gentlemen of Verona*. At the interval, he went for ice cream. There was a big queue, and I waited patiently in the foyer.

Natasha emerged from a group of teenagers clustered near the cloakroom. For a moment, I didn't recognise her. She'd cut her hair shorter and started wearing make-up again: just a little lipstick and blusher. Her legs were hidden by loose jeans and her sweater didn't flatter her figure.

Natasha saw me. I thought she'd turn away but she walked straight over. I couldn't understand why she'd want to talk to me, but I kept my cool.

'School trip?' I asked.

She nodded. 'Date?'

'No. Family outing.'

'Don't try it on with me, Caitlin. I saw him.'

'Oh.'

'Aaron said you might do something stupid like this, that you had this demon that came out sometimes.'

'I don't know what you're talking about,' I said.

Natasha gave me this infuriating, condescending, knowing smile. 'He lives on your street, doesn't he? You must be the exact age I was when he started working on me: so caring, so sorry he'd spread my pathetic little secret in a lesson. What did he tell you? How unfair it was that Aaron chucked you? How lonely he'd been feeling since he was unfairly suspended and his girlfriend dumped him?'

She thought I was going out with my own father. Before I could correct her, Natasha went on.

'It's not very comfortable, that fold-down bed in the camper van, is it? Don't worry. When he's sure of you, he'll take you to his house. Or maybe you've already been there. It's just along your street, isn't it?'

She had to be lying, I thought. But if she was lying, how did she know about the fold-down bed? I looked around. Dan was near the front of the queue. I had to speak quickly.

'If you were having an affair with him,' I said to her. 'Why did you make up those lies about him?'

'Because he finished it,' Natasha hissed. 'Last summer, one minute we were screwing like rabbits, every day. Another year and I thought it would be out in the open. He talked about me moving in with him. Then, two weeks before term starts, he says we have to cool it. The next week, he tells me not to call. We're too big a risk, it's over. He's sorry.'

I understood. Dan had stopped sleeping with her when Mum agreed that I could move in with him.

'You wanted revenge because he chucked you?'

'Yeah. Just like he'll chuck you when he gets tired of you. I chose my moment carefully, went to see Dan when I knew Michael was working outside the classroom. I'd seen him spying on us before. And I was all soppy with Dan: if it has to be that way it has to be and I gave him a great big kiss, before shouting at him and storming out. I popped a couple of buttons on the way, made sure Michael got an eyeful. I thought that'd be enough. I didn't realise teachers can get away with murder.'

I believed most of what she was saying. I didn't want to, but I did. Yet, for some stupid reason, I still felt the need to defend him.

'I think you made a move for Dan, not the other

way round,' I challenged. 'You knew he was vulnerable after Jo Grant left.'

Nat shook her head. 'I liked Ms Grant, but, the way he talked, I don't think he was all that into her. I reckon he was using her for cover. He likes them young. Me, I was getting too old. You're . . . what – barely fifteen. Just right for him. Half his age.'

'Less. He's thirty-six.'

'How did you find that out? I should have guessed the bastard lied about his age. He lied about everything else.'

Natasha was making my flesh crawl, but she wouldn't shut up.

'Dan acts kind, but he's a user. I wasn't the first, I'm sure of that. He hinted that there was one the year he taught in London. He probably used the act he used on me – softened her up for two terms then, in the summer, made his move.'

'No!' I looked over my shoulder. Dan was at the front of the queue. I spoke quickly. 'You ought to have given Aaron and me a chance,' I said. 'Instead of always being on at him, getting in between us.'

'Is that what you and Dan is about: revenge for me and Aaron?'

'You're with Aaron now?'

'I could be, if I chose to.'

'You can't choose who to love,' I said. 'Maybe you can only choose who not to love.'

'Then be sensible,' Natasha urged, her voice almost kind. 'Choose not to love Dan.'

'I can't do that.'

'You're sticking with him? You're mad.'

'I don't have any choice,' I said. 'He's my dad.'

Her mouth fell open and I left her, still standing there, in the foyer, with her back to my father.

'Who was that girl you were talking to?' Dan asked when I joined him.

'Just somebody from my old school.'

38

I hardly spoke on the drive home. Dan was prattling on about the play and didn't even notice the state I was in. I'd learned to hide my anger, to bury it. Not saying what was really on my mind had become second nature. But the anger was still there. Dan had lied to me, to everyone. Maybe he didn't think what he'd done was wrong. But it made me think of other things he'd done wrong, things I'd pushed to a dusty cupboard at the back of my mind.

Everybody lies, they tell me in counselling, even the people closest to you. But the worst lies aren't the ones you tell other people. They're the ones you tell yourself.

It occurred to me as he drove: Natasha wouldn't be able to keep the story to herself. She'd tell Aaron. Maybe I ought to tell him first. I could also tell him about Natasha and Dan. Aaron would discover we'd both deceived him, big time. Me reading his diary was kids' stuff compared to Natasha's affair with Dan. I wondered how he'd take it.

When we got home, I meant to get myself some juice to take upstairs. I was going to pack a suitcase, ready for the morning. I would leave the house before Dan got up, get a bus into town, then another one to Ashbourne, then another one to Parwich. I had nowhere else to go. As I was taking off my coat, Dan poured himself the big drink he always had at the end of the evening. After his first gulp, he said:

'I've got it.'

Stupidly, because I was ignoring him, I asked: 'Got what?'

'The girl you were talking to at The Crucible. I've been trying to work out who she reminded me of. Now I've got it: Natasha Clark, when I first taught her. Natasha used to have her hair short like that before she let it grow.'

He was so blasé, I couldn't help blurting out the truth.

'It was Natasha.'

'Right.' There was no surprise in his voice. He'd been testing me. Our eyes met. He knew that I knew.

'Can you guess what she thought was going on?'

Dan didn't answer. He was working out where this

might lead, and he didn't want to go there. Neither did I, so I went to my room. I had packing to do.

An hour later, just after I'd been to the loo. Dan pushed open my door without knocking. As he stumbled into the room, I pulled down the shirt I was wearing – an old shirt of his – until it covered my thighs. He didn't seem to notice the suitcase by the side of the bed.

'So she told you,' he said. I could smell the alcohol on him.

Dan was drunk. Not sociably, happily drunk the way he used to get when he lived with Mum. Dan was angrily, lasciviously drunk, the way he used to get after Mum left. I'd thought that side of him was long gone. If I hadn't believed he was a changed man, I'd never have come to live with him. Now I wished I'd locked my bedroom door the moment I got back from the bathroom.

'She told me,' I said.

'She thought you were my girlfriend.'

'Easy mistake to make,' I said, not looking him in the eye.

'There was a time when it wouldn't have been a mistake.'

When Dan said this, I flinched. We never spoke

about that. Three summers ago, just before my first period, I used to tell myself I had two dads: *bad Dad* and *good Dad*. I could deal with what bad Dad did when it only happened now and then. But that holiday was meant to last two whole weeks. Just the two of us, touring the seaside, in the camper van. After five days, I rang Mum, asked if I could come home. I said Dan was drunk all the time and it scared me.

The afternoon before Mum arrived, Dan promised he'd never, ever do it again. It wasn't him, he'd said, it was the drink. He'd begged me not to tell Mum. Of course I agreed – telling Mum was the last thing I wanted. I didn't know how to discuss stuff like that. I didn't want to put Dan in prison. I wanted him to stop getting into my bed every night and having sex with me.

'I want you out of my room.' My voice was dry, spluttery. Dan took a step back, into the doorway. I pulled the shirt I slept in more tightly around me. My father turned on the anguish. I folded my arms as he spurted out his apology.

'I used to feel so guilty,' he said towards the end. 'Even after I stopped drinking, at AA meetings I could never tell anyone what happened between us. It sounded too terrible.'

Then he said the worst thing, the thing that made me realise what he was really after.

'As for Natasha, I tried to hide from the truth. I didn't want to admit it to myself, or to you. I know you're hurt. I know I lied. But Cate, I swear – all the time I was with her, I was thinking of you.'

I wanted to vomit, but my throat was dry. Now I was sure of what he wanted. He thought I'd let him start it up again. He'd make me say I was enjoying it – *bad Cate* – the way he used to when I was twelve, and part of me believed him. I'd started to believe in him again, only now I knew better. People didn't change. *Good Dad* and *bad Dad*: they were one and the same.

That's when I lost it. I threw myself into the doorway. I meant to get past him, to get out of the house, but Dan wouldn't move. He just stood there. I kept pounding him with my fists. He didn't fight back. I don't know why – he was too drunk and ashamed or he was shocked because I was hitting him so hard.

Later, neighbours said they heard me screaming terrible things. I don't remember any of that. All I remember is Dan covering his chest, but not letting me past him. When I began to kick his shins, he took a couple of steps back, out of the doorway, onto the narrow landing.

'Let me go!' I tried to push round him and Dan took another step back. I lost my footing and grabbed the banister to hold me up. In front of me, Dan tried to stay upright but tripped on a stair. Falling backwards, he lost his balance. I watched him reach for the banister. He missed.

It was the banister rail he cracked his head on as he fell down the stairs, breaking his neck.

Epilogue

Mum had to sit with me during the police interviews. That's when she found out – about Natasha, and the rest. She still thinks she should have known what Dan did. Mum feels guilty and ashamed she didn't sense it. The mothers often do know, my counsellor says. They keep quiet because reporting the abuse will lead to more trouble than the abuse itself.

In the end, I wasn't prosecuted. The inquest verdict was accidental death. Since then, I've been getting professional help. I go to a counsellor social services set me up with. Mum saw a private counsellor for a while, too. These days, once a month, the two of us have sessions together with a third counsellor. Things are getting better between us.

I didn't go to Dan's funeral. Mum did. She told me Jo Grant was there, and a couple of teachers from the school in Sheffield. The teachers found what happened hard to believe, Mum said. One of them kept going on about how Dan came across as 'a wonderful, warm man, not one of those creepy saddos you see in the newspaper stories.'

'He was a good actor,' Mum told them. 'I don't know if any of us really knew him. I don't know if he really knew himself.'

When I moved to my new school, the teachers there offered to keep my past quiet. I wasn't having that. I've kept enough secrets. I don't make new friends easily, never have. But at least, here, I get respect. People know my story. You don't mess with a girl who killed her dad, accidentally or otherwise.

I haven't heard anything of Aaron. Or Natasha. I don't have a boyfriend at the moment. I don't even have any close friends. I can't pretend to be happy with my life. 'Give it time,' Mum said the other night. 'Teenage years are the toughest ones. Get through them and you can get through anything.'

She didn't realise what she'd just told me. No wonder I spend so much time in bed. According to her, I'm only halfway through the worst years of my life.

Wake me up when they're over.

If you've been affected by the issues in *Denial*, it can help to talk about it. Many schools have counsellors. Your local Samaritans will be in the phone book. Or you can ring Childline on 08001111.

visit www.davidbelbin.com

A note from the author

Thanks to Mandy, Mike, Paul,
Fran, Jenny, Penny, Sue, Eileen
and the Litcritters for assistance with
aspects of this novel.

Most of all, thanks to my editors,
Venetia Gosling and Emily Thomas.

David Belbin's previous Bite novels include
FESTIVAL and THE LAST VIRGIN.